A NOTE ON THE AUTHOR

Orlanda Marsden lives in South London with a cat and a partner and some grown-up children. She has been a teacher, poet, performer, dedicated recorder player and seller of crafty stuff at markets. She thinks her duty in life is to cook for everyone, when actually she should be writing.

Leaving England is her first novel.

Leaving England

Orlanda Marsden

Copyright © 2021: Orlanda Marsden

All rights reserved. No part of this book may be reproduced in any form or by any electronic or mechanical means, including information storage and retrieval systems, without permission in writing from the author.

ISBN: PB: 978-1-8382595-3-2

ISBN: eB: 978-1-8382595-4-9

Compilation & Cover Design by S A Harrison

Published by WriteSideLeft UK

https://www.writesideleft.com

1

Night. Police and ambulance vehicles belted up and down the roads, sirens wailing like creatures in pain.

No need for fear – they were out there to help. They were dealing with the Runners. There were laws in place now: no travel without good reason, no contact with strangers. Isolate yourself if you were ill. Though the illness itself seemed a good enough reason to travel, to get away from other people. She began to wonder if she ought to take the children away…

Sirens came screaming nearer. She lay, tense, hearing doors slamming and voices shouting. She forced herself out of bed to peer between the curtains. Ambulances and police cars stood outside the house opposite, harsh white lights flooding the street, blotting out the warm glow from the open front door. Mrs. Long stood in her worn old dressing-gown, wringing her hands and howling. Dark figures came out of the house carrying a covered stretcher, shoving the old woman out of the way. Then she was grabbed and pushed into one of the waiting cars.

Liz stumbled back to bed, horrified. Too near, this

time. As the room grew lighter, she fell into a fitful sleep.

Bells were ringing. Police? Ambulance again?

No, her mobile. She groped under the pillow.

"Michael?" He was the only person who'd phone in the night.

"Get away!" someone croaked. "Quick! Before it's too late!"

"Dad?" she asked. "Is that you, dad? What's the matter?"

"Get away!" he said, coughing and choking.

"Dad! Dad!" Liz shouted. "I'll come – wait!"

"It's too late – you've got to go! Your mother's gone…" and his voice trailed away.

"She's dead," she said, understanding.

"Got it last week. She's gone. Take those kids and get out of here."

"But what about…?"

"Don't worry about me – I'll be gone soon. I know the signs. Go now, while you still can…"

The line went dead.

Liz leaned back against her pillow, tears running down her cheeks. She wondered how and when to tell the children. But first she had to make plans.

She shook Ben awake, calling out to Kate as she went. "Up! Breakfast in two minutes! Hurry! Now!" She heard Ben grumbling, and Kate skipping about deciding which bits of uniform were least crumpled.

She laid the table. She ate a handful of dry cereal –

leave the milk for the children – and sipped some tea as they clattered into the kitchen.

"Not allowed!" said Kate, hearing her mother crunching but seeing no bowl.

"Can I have eggs?" asked Ben.

The eggs were for supper, "Yes, of course!" she answered, pleased that he wanted to eat.

"Where's Daddy?" Kate asked suddenly. "Is he up?"

"Don't be so stupid," growled Ben. "He went ages ago."

"I expect he is up," said Liz carefully. "No need to be so cross, Ben."

There was every need to be cross – furious. "Look," Michael had said one evening several weeks back, "I'm thinking of staying in the office. It'll make more sense to be near the centre of things, and I won't risk infection by travelling. I'll be able to let you know what's going on…"

That was the last they had heard from him. "What about us? What about the children?" she'd wanted to scream. She was left facing what she'd always suspected, that Michael's job came before his love of family.

"Come on, come on!" she hustled them. "Hairbrush, toothbrush, pee!" A mantra she'd repeated since they were tiny, and Ben showed no signs yet that he didn't need reminding. Michael thought she shouldn't still be driving him to school. "You'll make him into a real wimp. What if he does bunk off now and then? – all kids do!" Liz thought, but didn't say, that in these times it was better to be sure he arrived safely. Anyway, he came home by himself.

She drove to the local supermarket. There were signs in large uneven letters telling you to take no more than two of anything. Civilised women like herself raced to grab the last tin of ham or peach halves. She pushed the trolley round, picking up tins – beans, vegetables, corned beef, even Spam.

She remembered her parents and grandparents telling her about the war – potato-peeling and cabbage-stalk soup. She'd read the books and seen the films: people shared, got together, helped each other out. The enemy was the scream of an aeroplane, the whine of a bomb, fires and explosions. You had a bit of a chance: run, hide and save people. Now, the people you loved best presented the greatest danger.

She found her allowance of tinned and dry goods, and picked up some frozen chicken and vegetables – peas, sweetcorn, and spinach. Beneath tired signs labelled "Fresh Fruit 'n' Veg" crouched apologetic-looking wrinkled carrots and parsnips, greening potatoes, and wilted cabbages. She supposed supply lorries had difficulty getting through, or, worse, crops weren't being grown or harvested or picked any more. She could make soup – not a favourite with either child, but comfort food for Liz, like the cawl, the Welsh stew, her mother used to make. Wales, where for years they'd holidayed with the children in her parents' old house. Until Michael had grown too grand for it and taken them to hotter, smarter places. But Wales was special – and safe.

Back home, she hunted for picnic boxes and other sturdy containers, piling the shopping and the contents of the fridge and freezer into them. Before she picked the children up from school, she would pack the car with everything she thought they'd need.

Kate's stuff was easy. Liz tipped everything – party dress and shoes included – into a plastic dustbin bag. She picked up the grimy bit of rag, what remained of Kate's baby blanket, never washed. She added books – Alice, Grimms' Fairy tales, and *The Wind in the Willow*s, which she might grow into. Ben still liked it. In Ben's room, she chose *Boy's Book of Woodcraft*, and the complete Sherlock Holmes. What about his computer? All those hideous warfare games that he played, loudly and late, with his friends. Too bad.

Her choices were easy: practical clothes and underwear – none of the dresses and flimsies she had bought for her role as the boss's wife. She emptied the bathroom cupboard of soaps, toothpaste and shampoo into a sponge bag, filled another with essentials such as Tampax, elastoplasts, bandages, and any medicines she could find – aspirin and paracetamol, Calpol and Benylin. A thermometer, and nail scissors. She paused at her expensive face creams, deciding instead on a nearly-full bottle of Nivea. Her mother had always used Nivea.

Back in the kitchen she dug out plastic shopping

bags, and packed all the tinned food she could find, groping for the tinned mandarin oranges and mushy peas from the back of the cupboard. Rice, pasta, lentils and pearl barley. Cleaning stuff from under the sink went in to a large "Bag for life" – bleach, soda crystals she had never used, washing-up liquid, squirty stuff for surfaces, and finally Jay-cloths, and the end of a roll of bin-liners.

Finally, the sitting-room. Nothing there, surely? She eyed the room – mostly Michael's taste; he never had liked her choices. She wouldn't miss the Knole sofa, nor the shiny damask curtains… ah, the desk! She scuffled round for their passports, medical and birth certificates. Not Michael's. Did he always carry his passport with him? She ignored her laptop – it probably wouldn't work for much longer. Then she noticed the drinks' cabinet, and grabbed an unopened bottle of brandy. Medicinal.

What was the time? She started to load the car, hiding the bin bags as far as possible under the supermarket shopping.

She jammed the last shopping bag into the boot.

"Going anywhere nice?" said a loud voice.

Liz jumped, and turned. Rodney, her neighbour. "Because you can't go far in these times," he said smugly. "It's been on the news, you know – can't go further than a shopping trip – 'No journey without purpose.'"

"Well, I have been shopping, and now we're just going… to see my parents for a few days."

"Not poorly, are they?" he asked, backing away.

"No, no," she lied. "Just getting older – need a bit of support, you know. You could keep an eye on the house for me, if you wouldn't mind – be a weight off my mind."

Rodney nodded importantly. "Be only too glad," he said. "Leave us a phone number and I can get in touch. Mother and I can both keep a weather eye out for you."

They exchanged numbers. She didn't much like him, but he had caught her red-handed. His mother was a constant and shadowy shape behind her nets, so could be useful. And who knew how long phones were going to last, anyway?

She made one last check that all the doors and windows were locked, even the internal doors, then remembered something. She dashed back to the children's rooms and bundled up their duvets and pillows, which she spread out over the car's back seat.

Rodney lingered on his doorstep and waved. "Safe journey!" he called, loudly.

2

Liz drove to Kate's school first. She walked in to the foyer; the strict security was gone. A large notice said, "Please disinfect your hands here." She squirted the strong-smelling stuff into one palm and rubbed it thoroughly all over her hands. Miss McCarthy watched her from the office.

"I've just come to pick up Kate," she said. "We've got a…"

"That's what they all say," Miss McCarthy interrupted. "Medical or home-schooling – that's what they say. Won't have any kids left, soon. You don't want to see the Head, do you?" she added. "Only she's feeling the pressure a bit, at the moment." She made a curious gesture with her hand, which Liz at first took to be a wave, then understood was shorthand for drinking.

She hurried down the corridor to Kate's classroom. No children argued over the home corner or the lego; the atmosphere was subdued, children wandering round being quiet and good in their strangely spacious surroundings.

"Kate, Mummy's here!" called Mrs. Robinson.

"We have to go now," Liz told her, smiling at the teacher. Mrs. Robinson gave the slightest of shrugs, Kate dragged herself reluctantly away from Nancy, her best friend of the moment, and waved goodbye to the class. Then they were back in the car.

"Where are we going, Mum?" Kate asked. "It's not home-time. And I was playing with Nancy."

"We're going to pick up Ben, and then we're going on an adventure!"

"And are we going home then?" Kate asked.

"No," said Liz. "We're going on a kind of holiday," she ventured.

"I haven't packed!"

"I have," said Liz

There was silence for a while.

"Mummy, did you pack Blonk?"

"Yes, of course I did – it was the first thing I put in!"

Kate sighed in relief. That was all right, then. "And did you pack my new anorak?" she asked. "And my blue furry jumper? And my sticking-out skirt with the flowers? And my glitter t-shirt?"

This went on a while, Liz murmuring "Mmm," and "Of course."

It was a journey she had done every day for two years, and to begin with it had taken almost an hour to get through the traffic. Now the roads were empty, except for the police cars and ambulances and their noise. People were at last taking notice of the advertisements everywhere: "No journey without purpose. Never drive when you can walk." Well, she couldn't walk to Ben's school, and neither could he. She refused to feel guilty about driving.

As she approached Ben's school she saw why there was so little traffic. There was a road block ahead of them. Police – good god, were they armed? – were stopping all vehicles. But she had her driving licence, and she was only picking up her son from school…

She opened her window.

"Sorry, Madam – I'm afraid you can't go any further."

"I'm just going to pick my son up from school – he has a dental appointment, you see, so – "

"And then we're going on holiday!" said a cheerful voice. Liz cursed herself for presenting the police as friendly helpers in times of trouble.

"Oh, maybe later," said Liz, trying to laugh it off. "We've got to pick up Ben, then we'll go home and make dinner together."

"You do seem to have quite a bit of shopping," said the policeman stolidly, eyeing the piled boot. She hoped the bin bags were well hidden.

"So can we go now? It's only a bit further on – the Royal Sadler's School, you know." If she had hoped the name of the school would impress him, she was wrong.

"This is as far as anyone can go, Madam. The surrounding area is closed off. Now, if you wouldn't mind turning round and going back where you came from, there are other people…"

In the driving mirror she could see just one car

behind them. "But my son! I have to get him!" She found she was weeping and then felt warm arms round her neck.

"Mummy! Don't cry, Mummy – let's go home now. I don't like this adventure."

Liz struggled to control herself. "It's all right, my love – don't worry! We'll go back and wait for Ben to come home."

The policeman shifted his gun in an embarrassed manner. "I'm afraid no one can leave this area, either, Madam. I can assure you that your boy is better off where he is – safer, if you see what I mean." He jerked his head towards Kate, who was still clinging round her mother's neck.

"But he's only fourteen! He must come home!"

Kate was crying. "I want Ben! Why can't we get him, Mummy?"

"It's all right, sweetheart – we'll find him. We'll do it later, okay? Don't cry." She wanted to wail and scream. She sniffed and rubbed her face, and tried to smile. Another policeman was striding towards them.

"Problems?" the new one asked.

"Nah..." said the first. "Madam's just going to take her little girl home again, aren't you, Madam?"

Liz wanted to punch the fool on the nose. How could he expect her to leave her son? The two uniformed men peered into the car. It'd be safer to leave without more drama. She didn't want to attract too much attention. She nodded at them, swung the car round and drove away.

"But, mummy!" wailed Kate.

"Wait!" Liz hissed, and once round a bend in the road, turned right, driving as fast as she dared before turning right again. There must be safe way. She went down a long tree-lined road of solid Victorian houses.

"Mummy! Mum!" Kate's voice was insistent. "Are we going the right way?"

"I hope so," said Liz. "Look, just down the road there, that's where the playing fields begin. Perhaps we can get in that way."

She parked right by the playing fields' gate. It was locked with a heavy chain and padlock.

"Okay," she said. "Now comes the adventurous bit! Are you coming?" It was surely better to take Kate with her than to leave her alone. Even though there was nobody about. Especially since there was nobody was about.

They looked at the gate.

"It's too high," said Kate.

She was right – even if they had climbed on the car to get over, they'd never be able to climb back out.

"What shall we do – oh god – what shall we do?"

"We could go round the front, Mummy – that's where we usually go in."

"You are so sensible, Katy!" Liz said. It might be worth a try.

In the car again, she crept along, looking for another place to get in. All gates and gaps were well and truly blocked, and recently, by the look of the new metal and wood of the locks and barriers. Kate's face pressed a cloudy patch on the window as she searched, too.

I hope she thinks it's a game, Liz was thinking, when suddenly Kate shouted.

"Look! There's the front door! And it's playtime!"

Liz slid to a halt and turned off the engine. "Come on!" she ordered. "Let's go and see what the boys play at recess."

"Playtime," corrected Kate.

"They call it recess in big schools," said Liz, putting her face against the railings. "See if you can spot Ben."

Boys were hurtling and fighting and kicking balls as she supposed they did every day. They seemed cheerfully oblivious to the dangerous times they were in. One or two boys waved at them – were they Ben's friends? – she couldn't see at this distance. A wild game of football that had started in the centre of the yard, gathered players and speed as the group scuffed and pushed its way towards the railings where Liz and Kate stood.

"Hi there! You looking for someone?" called a voice Liz did not know.

The game seethed and huddled closer to the railings.

"We're looking for my brother," said Kate, before Liz could speak

"Yes, Ben Patterson. Do you know where he is?"

"Fetch Patty!" ordered one of the players, without ceasing to hustle for the ball. A small figure streaked across the yard, to return moments later with Ben.

"Get the ball, Patty!" shouted a voice. Her son

bounced the ball a few times before it was grabbed from him, and Ben was pushed up against the railings.

"What are you doing here?" he asked, amazed. She couldn't tell if he was pleased or deeply embarrassed.

"We've come to take you away – we have to get out of London!"

"We're going on holiday," Kate shrieked, jumping up and down.

"To Grandpa and Grandma's? Are they coming, too?"

"Well, no – they're too ill… but we're going to Wales, and we've come…"

Ben's face changed. A Master was walking towards the heaving group.

"Come on, you boys – back in the yard. Now!"

"Mum, they won't let us out – the Head said someone in school's ill – I can't come home!"

The master reached him and shoved him roughly back into the thinning football game.

"Get away!" said the Master, glaring at Liz. "I'll have to call the police if I see you again. It's people like you who put everyone at risk!"

"What does he mean?" asked Kate.

Liz aimed for truth. "He thinks that we might spread the disease and he's frightened. And listen, Kate, that's – that's why we can't take Ben with us just now – it's too dangerous."

She was shaking as she turned to open the car and let Kate in, but Kate stayed where she was, a wooden post.

"We can't go without Ben," she said.

"We have to," said Liz quietly.

"I'm staying here!" Kate began to shriek. "I'm not going – shan't get in the car…!"

Liz picked Kate up and posted her head first, still screaming, on to the back seat. "We have to go. Ben will come and find us."

"But how will he know the way?" Kate cried.

"He's a clever boy – he'll find us. And we've been to Wales so many times." Liz hugged Kate, and they cried together as Liz rocked the child in her arms. Kate sobbed a last little hiccup. Tissues were found, noses blown, and eyes wiped. Liz rearranged the duvet and pillows and helped Kate to belt herself in.

"If anyone asks, we've just been shopping," she told Kate, as she drove towards the centre of town and the M4.

Kate giggled, looking at the stuff piled in the back. "I went to Lidl," she began, "and I bought a tin of beans and some jelly babies…"

"I went to Lidl," Liz continued, "and I bought a tin of beans, some jelly babies, and a box of chocolates…"

Kate's voice slowed, until she fell asleep.

3

Liz had thought of the Welsh house as soon as her father had told her to get away. Wales was the place of her childhood, where her parents had grown up and where she was born. They'd kept the house in the family ever since, spent school holidays there – a place of rain and beaches and soft air. Even Michael had liked it. Now she wondered what sort of welcome they'd get, whether they'd be regarded as incomers and refugees, instead of as the family of Tom Lloyd Jones.

She drove on through West London, with its houses and mansion flats set back from the road. Ambulances and police cars overtook them, sirens wailing; there was little other traffic. Perhaps people were shutting themselves away to sit it out; perhaps they had already left. Perhaps there weren't many people left….

"Look, Mummy – a fox! And another! " said Kate. She hadn't slept long.

Mangy animals slunk along the pavement. "I think they're dogs, actually," she said to Kate.

"But why are they out all by themselves?"

"Just going for a walk, I expect," said Liz.

"Silly! They don't do that! I think they're looking for dinner."

"I expect you're right," Liz replied, surprised again by her daughter's easy acceptance of the strangeness. There had been warnings about feral dogs in the media, illustrated with dramatic photographs and film footage. Liz had seen a pack herself once, as she was dropping Ben off at school, a mixture of breeds, all loping along, intent and ferocious. She wouldn't let Kate out of her sight.

She put the radio on, to quell bad thoughts. Dogs, Ben, Mum and Dad, the village…

"… here is Nicholas Chorley reading it." News. She made to turn it off in case Kate asked questions she didn't want to answer. Then listened. "In the interests of public safety, the government requests that travel shall be limited to no more than five miles per day. Petrol will be rationed accordingly."

Rationing. She must fill the car as soon as they got on the motorway. What if the motorways were closed? Perhaps only emergency services and delivery lorries were allowed to use them.

They were passing the Fullers' Brewery, and there was the roundabout and a sign to the M4 and the West.

It wasn't closed. Lorries and vans in abundance, not many cars. Hope I don't get stopped, she thought desperately, turning on to the motorway.

"I'm really hungry, Mummy. Can we have breakfast on the motorway?" It had been their ritual to start the holiday journey early and have a deliciously unhealthy fry-up in a service station.

"I'm not sure there's anywhere open," said Liz cautiously.

"But I'm so starving – it must be dinner time. And I didn't eat my lunch at school."

"Well, that's your fault," said Liz sharply. "Okay, okay – we'll stop at the next one and see," she added.

They drove for a while in silence, Kate watchful for signs. "There's one!" she shouted.

"But there are no lights on," Liz pointed out. She was disappointed, too – she needed a pee and coffee, and petrol, if she was to drive on. "Let's try the next one."

It was a long way before Kate spotted one that was lit. There were eerily few people about. "Stay by me," Liz said

"But can't I go and play…"

"No!" Liz snapped. "Just because!" she added, as Kate began to object.

They went to the loo together. There were large notices everywhere exhorting you to wash your hands PROPERLY! Which they did, with Kate complaining at the smell of the disinfectant.

They went to the café.

"There's no one here!" said Kate, surprised.

"Well, it is evening now," said Liz. "Let's go and see what they've got to eat."

"I want breakfast," said Kate, a stickler for tradition.

Breakfast was off.

"You can have chicken and chips or egg and chips," said a surly woman behind the counter.

They ordered one of each, so they could share. "But I'm eating all my own chips," Kate said. Liz ordered coffee – "Macchiato, please."

"It's just coffee," snarled the woman.

Kate was allowed Coke.

As they came to pay, Liz suddenly wondered if she had enough money. Fancy launching on this journey without checking her purse, and her account!

"Mummy! You must give the man the money," Kate said patiently.

"That'll be fifteen pounds, sixty-five," he said.

"Do you take cards?" Liz asked. Then she must find a cash point and see… She handed the man her card. The machine was slow.

"Going far?" he asked pleasantly.

"Not very," she hedged, hoping Kate wouldn't contradict her.

"We've just been shopping," Kate said, playing the game too well.

"Funny place to shop," said the man, handing the card back.

"Oh, we've just been to…" Where the hell were they? She had no idea.

"Swindon!" shouted Kate in triumph.

Good god! – were they really that far along already? "Yes, Swindon."

"How on earth did you know?" she asked Kate in amazement while they ate.

"I can read," Kate said scathingly. "There was a big sign."

"Well, you are the number one best travelling companion!" Liz said.

"Better than Ben?" Kate asked in a small voice.

"As good as," said Liz firmly. Kate was putting leftover chips into her paper napkin and making a little parcel of them. "You can leave them if you're too full – it doesn't matter."

"I'm keeping them for Ben," Kate replied. "He always likes meals on the motorway."

"Put them in your rucksack, then," was all she said.

She filled up the car at the petrol pump. The man at the desk was furious. "Don't you know about rationing?" he growled.

"I'm so sorry!" she said, lying. "I quite forgot!" Which was almost true, and he could hardly take the petrol out of the car now.

"Some people think they own the world," he muttered. "I could report you to the authorities." As he handed her the receipt, she slid a ten-pound note under the glass. He took it without a word and pushed it into his pocket with a practised air. Liz walked away before Kate could ask why.

"Why did you pay the man twice, Mummy?" Kate asked as they got in the car.

"I didn't," said Liz.

"But you gave him..." Kate began.

"It was a sweetener!" said Liz in desperation.

"I'd like a sweetener," said Kate. "Chocolate – a whole bar!"

"You'll have to wait till we stop again."

They left the cheerful lights of the Leigh Delamere Service Station, and drove on and on without stopping. Kate forgot about chocolate, sang quietly to herself, and invented long and complicated stories under her breath.

"Wales," she announced to Kate, who just nodded and went on with her story.

Liz had always loved arriving – "The bridge! The bridge!" the children used to shout, knowing the journey was half over.

Daylight was fading. Poor Ben, she was thinking, What else could she have done? She thought of her father and his warning – just that morning. She had to take Kate away from all that. How long was the incubation period? Were they safe? Dad was probably dead by now... She tasted tears in her throat, and hoped he would be found quickly and dealt with. Whatever that meant. She was so tired. Her eyes kept flickering shut, opening again with a jerk of her neck.

"Port Talbot," said Kate, without looking up.

"How do you know?"

"It smells funny."

She lost concentration again. This was stupid. You didn't flee the plague in London only to die in a car crash. The Cardiff bypass was behind them. We'll just get through Carmarthen, then I have to stop, she thought. "Kate! Are you still awake? Sing to me!"

Obediently Kate started their repertoire of car songs – "My old man's a dustman," "Where have you been all the day?" and "Que sera, sera". They sang loudly, leaving the town and sliding along narrow roads, where sudden turns and overhanging branches and occasional blinding headlights kept her alert. And the singing, of course.

There was a small lay-by, dark with trees. She pulled over and parked as close to the bordering hedges as she could. In her headlights she saw that one end of the lay-by was occupied by a motorised caravan. Painted on one side: "Best Hotdogs In The West!!!" and "Chips With Everything!!!" There was a worn notice flapping over the hatch – a makeshift menu. The van had an abandoned air. Even if it were still in use, no one would cook at night.

A sleepy voice said, "Mummy, I want a hotdog."

"They're closed," said Liz.

"Why did we stop, then?" Kate asked reasonably.

"Because I'm really tired and about to fall asleep, and this seems a quiet place." Liz leaned into the back and dragged one of the duvets and a pillow towards her.

"Now I'm all cold," Kate whined.

Liz slammed out of the car, and rearranged both duvets. "All right?" she asked, and Kate snuggled down again and closed her eyes. Then Liz poked a pillow into the gap round the gear stick, and spread a duvet across the two front seats, placing her handbag as neck support.

Eventually she slept.

It was daylight when she woke, stiff and uncomfortable, with a pain in her side where the gear lever had dug in. "Mummy!" Kate was saying. "Mummy! Wake up! There's a man!"

Liz sat up suddenly, trying to rub the sleep from her eyes. She slid over to the driver's seat and opened the door.

There was a man, a man in uniform. "Bore da," he said without a smile.

"Bore da," said Liz politely. "What's the matter?"

"Ah, you don't speak our language, then."

"Not really," Liz replied. "And the problem is…?"

"The problem is, what you're doing is illegal." Liz wondered which bit of what she was doing he was talking about – leaving her son? Leaving her dead and dying parents? Abandoning her home? Driving?

"Lay-bys are for emergency use only. Says so on the notice."

"Well, it was a sort of emergency," said Liz. "I got very tired driving, so I thought I'd better stop, for safety's sake."

"We've just been shopping," said Kate helpfully, smiling through her opened window.

"Funny place to sleep," he said. "Home for breakfast?"

"Yes, I'm hungry," Kate said.

God, anyone would think I'd trained her, Liz thought, smiling.

"Better be on your way, then – don't want to keep you. Just you remember now, next time, Mam!" he nodded meaningfully at Liz. "Bore da!"

"Bore da!" Kate called, closing her window and waving. "He was a nice man, wasn't he, Mummy?"

"Yeah – yes, I expect so," said Liz, still bemused. "Okay – breakfast it is! Keep your eyes peeled for anywhere that looks open."

The last leg of the journey took them along a narrow tree-lined road bordering the River Teifi. Not breakfast-café terrain.

"We could stop in Newcastle Emlyn," said Kate.

"Well, we could," said Liz. "But we're so near – it might be better to press on. And then we can have a super-special fry-up, just the two of us!"

"Two," said Kate. "Yes, okay."

So, through Cardigan, over the River Teifi, and right to the village.

Home. Soft sea-salt air filled their lungs. Liz opened the front door. The familiar smell of age and damp and disuse greeted them. Liz turned on the water and the heating, and opened some windows. "Do you want to light a fire?" It was another ritual, the lighting of the wood, and the first meal.

"Kate?" She heard her running up and down stairs, out of the front door, glimpsed her going round the back of the house. "Kate!"

She appeared at the kitchen door, her face white and tear-stained.

"Whatever's the matter?" Liz grabbed her.

Kate pulled violently away. "You said he'd find us!" she wailed.

Liz groped back through their conversations.

"At his school," Kate cried. "You said he was clever and he'd find us!"

"I didn't mean…" Liz began. "I meant eventually…" Her voice rose in frustration. "I mean, don't be so stupid – look how long it's taken us to get here by car! How ever do you think he could beat us to it…?" She tried to laugh. Kate flung herself away and on to the sofa, head under the cushions.

"But you said! I didn't want to come, but you said!" And then – "Why did you go without him?" she shrieked, sobbing and choking until she could barely breathe.

Liz went to hug her again but Kate lashed out, catching her painfully on the nose.

"Stop it!" Liz shouted through tears. "Don't you dare hit me! And stop making that dreadful noise – you're not a baby! Listen," she went on more quietly, "I explained – I told you we had to go quickly, because of this disease – we didn't have time to wait for Ben…"

"We didn't even say goodbye to Nan…"

Now Liz thumped down next to Kate and put her arms tightly round her. "Listen. Gramps told me we had to go, because Nan got so ill. And she died… And he was going to get it next… do you see? I know it's horrible – everything is so upside down at the moment. Ben will come soon, I'm sure…"

Kate had quietened. "I wanted Nan and Gramps with us, too…" she sniffed.

"So did I, my love," said Liz, stifling tears in Kate's hot neck.

Later, she would think how odd it was that Kate hadn't mentioned her father. Or perhaps not – he had always been for Sunday best, not everyday use. Both children were used to turning to her for praise and for problems; it wasn't that they had cut Michael out: he had removed himself – home late, meetings, courses – seldom time to listen, let alone talk.

"Come on, now," Liz said, pulling herself back to the present. "Let's get ourselves sorted, so we're ready when Ben does come."

They lit the fire – Kate loved making the newspaper snails to balance the wood on – and heaved the stuff out of the car. Liz unpacked the food and put it away, trying to cram all the perishables into the small fridge and freezer, while Kate lugged bin bags up the stairs and into the bedrooms.

Then Liz made "breakfast", while Kate slammed drawers and doors in her room upstairs.

"I've unpacked," she announced, coming downstairs at last. Apart from some redness round the eyes, she looked more herself, and was hungry.

Sorting and unpacking went on for several days. Liz

put out a milk bottle that she found under the sink one day, and next day there was a fresh pint. Then she put a little note out – "No milk today, but could we have a large loaf and half of butter?" And magically, there they were. The milkman left a hand-written leaflet – he could also deliver orange juice, bacon, eggs and his wife's home-baked Welsh cakes. No need to brave the village supermarket yet a while.

Eventually all the bin bags were unpacked and clothes put away; spare bedding was taken out of the chests and aired in the garden. Liz began to wash the curtains and the old Welsh quilts that had lain on each bed ever since she could remember. Kate made a camp in the garden, using frayed sheets across a branch of the apple tree. She spent hours inside her flapping white tent with a pile of Liz's childhood books that she'd discovered in the cupboard under the stairs.

Liz, taking up the dirty, flowered carpet in the living-room, discovered beneath it handsome slate flagstones. She found rag rugs in the bedrooms, which she beat vigorously to expel years of dust, and arranged them on the flags. The room looked cosy and brighter: the old curtains hung in thick folds, framing the view of the river's shining expanse. With every change, Liz remembered her parents; how her mother had made cushions for the sofa out of bits of their old dresses; how her father had fixed the phone to the wall with a special hook for a message pad and pencil; how Mum had always slept with the curtains open, " to see the view", and Dad had always taken the cane armchair out to the front of the house, "to watch the people go by." Liz was beginning to feel at home.

Whatever she did, Ben was in her mind – escaping from school, walking along the hard shoulder of the motorway, hiking across country, getting lifts… Both children knew about lifts and strangers – surely he would be safe? Would anyone be brave enough to pick him up? Hitching, like handshaking, was probably a thing of the past.

Kate often asked when Ben would arrive.

"Soon," Liz would say. It was easier to drift along. But from time to time, Kate could be spotted, coming out of her latest tent, scanning the road up and down past the house.

4

Ben hated being a boarder. Worst of all, his school had no communication with the outside. Mobile phones were confiscated; laptops could no longer connect to the internet. Some boys thought their mobiles didn't work because all the masts were down, and the internet had disappeared because bandwidth was preserved for those in government. The problem was that nobody knew. They were all getting twitchy because they couldn't play computer games, or contact friends or family, nor was there any way of establishing the facts about the virus. Television and radio repeated the same bland warnings about hygiene, and promised a speedy end to the problem. Ben and his friends jeered when they heard the Government platitudes.

After lessons and homework, the boys were herded into the common-room or the library and left to themselves. They argued constantly over the computers for game-playing, and the television, though there was nothing worth watching, just the usual political and medical stuff, and an occasional old film. They all knew that someone in the school was dying. They had been told by the Headmaster at a frightening assembly. "If you are not careful and obedient, the disease might easily spread further within these very walls."

Ben rather hoped it was one of the masters who was infected. He pictured the one who sent his mother and sister away, threatening them with the police. That one would do.

He remembered them walking back to the car, and his mother's half-turn towards him before he was pulled roughly from the railings. One of his mates told him he'd seen the girl screaming and refusing to leave. He wished desperately they could have left together. He dragged his misery around with him in a great grey cloud.

He spent his time in lessons dreaming up escape plans.

From classroom windows and the grounds, he started looking for breaches in security. It was like a video game – watch and evaluate, weigh up the chances – but he was playing alone. The main doors were constantly guarded, and the railings circling the grounds were too high and exposed. Anyone climbing would be spotted immediately.

Then he realised he was stupidly imagining a daytime escape. He'd have to go at night, of course. So he began a series of night-time explorations. While the boys in the crowded room dormitory slept, he crept out of bed and wandered round the corridors, glad that Matron had kitted him out – as she had all the day boys – with the regulation striped pyjamas. As a day boy, he knew little about the layout of the sleeping arrangements, but there were small dim lights along the skirting boards, showing odd little staircases here and there, leading into dormitories, or classrooms pressed into emergency use for that purpose. The passages turned at odd angles, until Ben had no idea which way he was facing, and sometimes only by luck found his way back to bed before the morning bell rang.

He searched for signs to make his ramblings easier. Many passages were lined with long photographs of sports' teams in unfashionably long shorts, or the whole school from times long before Ben was born. There were paintings, too – dreary views of the school, portraits of long-ago headmasters. And once he was terrified to come face to face with another boy – his reflection in a glass vitrine containing sports' cups and shields. He began to remember the layout: pass a painting of school and a couple of headmasters, then turn left. That brought him to the beginning of his corridor.

Vigilant as he was, he was caught several times by a patrolling master. "Just going to the loo, Sir," he had blurted the first time.

"Where's your dormitory?" the master demanded.

"Down there, Sir," and Ben waved a hand, and that had seemed to be enough.

Another time he'd met the same master. "Something wrong with your bladder, Patterson?"

"No, Sir – I'm new here, Sir," Ben said. The master stared, then turned away.

Next time, someone else caught him. Ben avoided all eye-contact, kept walking, in spite of the master's calls. He was followed as he plodded back to the dormitory, followed by the master, who watched as Ben got into bed still wearing his slippers. Ben felt him standing there, staring, and kept his eyes closed.

Next morning Ben was called in to see the Head of House.

"Anything wrong, Patterson?"

"No, Sir," Ben hung his head. How stupid to get himself noticed!

"Only there have been reports, you know... Have you had problems with sleep-walking before?"

Ben shook his head.

"Anything wrong at home? Parents all right? Haven't had the pleasure of meeting your father – all OK?"

Ben knew full well that his father never did parents' evenings – "Your mother's better at that sort of thing," he'd always said. And he was usually too busy. "It's fine," he mumbled.

"It's a difficult time for all of us, Patterson, a bad time. We all need to work together, and put our personal feelings aside…"

"Yes, Sir. Sorry, Sir," Ben said, and was dismissed.

He took greater care not to be found. He learnt how to melt into an alcove, face to the wall, or duck down a staircase, to vanish. He ranged further in his investigations, from the kitchens – where he had disturbed rattling cockroaches, and once a long black rat – to the attics, piled with old cupboards and desks and out-of-date text books. One night at the end of a long corridor in a distant wing, he saw a noticeboard with a skull and cross bones painted on it – "DANGER – KEEP OUT" the writing said. Ben paused for a moment, then, hearing the door on the other side of a screen thud open, scuttled the long way back to his bed. He lay there panting.

It was true, then. The boys joked about it. "Sir! Sir! Johnson sneezed all over me – he's given me the plague! Oh, I'm dying, Sir – can I go home now?

But it wasn't funny, it was real.

Ben stopped his night wanderings. He needed to sleep. He was dozing through too many lessons, especially afternoon ones, and people were beginning to notice. One or two of his friends would nudge him as a master approached.

"If you can't be bothered to pay attention, Patterson, kindly get out of my class. And where's your homework? You seemed to manage it when you were a day boy!"

"Patty's gone batty!" someone hissed, and the class started giggling.

Ben kept his head down, avoiding eye contact. The escape had to be soon.

By now he knew where. There was a corner of the grounds, near the tennis courts, where there were a couple of benches under some trees; the trees overhung a wall, beyond which were gardens of houses backing on to the school.

It took him a few more days, watching, assessing, to build up his courage. He started playing a game of bounce against the wall with an old tennis ball he had found in the long grass. "Girly game, girly game," his mates jeered, and left him alone. That suited him. Plenty of time to decide which tree was easiest to climb and overhung furthest into neighbouring gardens.

The next problem was how to get out of school at night. He pictured his pillow lying body-like under the blankets, while he tiptoed out of the dormitory. But then what? How could he get out of the actual building? He spent more days wandering round the school in recess. His friends became used to him going off on his own.

Then he decided.

He went to bed as usual, but hid his clothes under the bedclothes with him. Slowly and carefully, he took off his pyjamas, and pulled on his daytime clothes, including shoes, but minus the bulky blazer with its incriminating school badge. He put his pyjamas back on over the top.

"What the fuck are you up to?" hissed the boy in the next bed.

"Just wants to prove he's still alive," said another voice.

Ben said nothing, but lay in the dark, hot and blushing. He waited until the muttering died down and there was a sound of steady breathing, and edged awkwardly out of bed. If anyone saw him now they would think he was going for a pee. The school was silent. He found his way down to the kitchens, where he had spotted a window in the staff loos that seemed to be always left open.

And he scrambled out.

Only to find himself in a closed courtyard, where the moon reflected dimly off the surrounding windows.

He hurtled round the space like a caged animal, shaking windows, rattling at doors, tripping over the rough paving, careless of secrecy. The window he had slithered out of was too high to reach from the outside, though he tried until his arms ached and his face was grazed with the effort.

He gave up, eventually. Found himself a corner by what looked like fire doors, curled up on the step, and fell into an uncomfortable sleep.

He was awoken violently when someone inside flung the doors open, and he was shoved off the step.

"Hey!" a voice exclaimed. "What you up to here?"

The man was wearing the white jacket and checked trousers of a cook. It was no use pretending to look for a loo, nor to be sleep-walking…

"Got lost," he mumbled stupidly.

The cook reached out and pulled him into the passage way. "You run away, no?"

"No!" Ben said emphatically.

"Yes, you try." The cook pulled at the edge of Ben's shirt where it showed under his pyjamas.

"No," said Ben again.

The cook cuffed Ben's head and pushed him along the corridor. "You go," he said. As Ben stared in amazement, the cook pushed him harder. "You, stupid boy! Go now! Away!"

He ran along the corridor until he came to the hall and the back stairs. Back to the dormitory where the others were just going down to breakfast.

"Come on, Patty – you're going to be late."

"Can I eat your breakfast if you don't want it?"

"Bags I his bacon!"

No one noticed when Ben took his pyjamas off and appeared ready dressed.

It was several days before Ben worked up the courage to try again. The window had been useless, but fire doors, now… They were made to be opened from the inside. He had noticed most of them were locked with heavy padlocks. But some of them must surely be usable, otherwise they would all fry to death. Fire… and an idea kindled.

Next day, after maths, Ben approached Robinson.

"Whatcher want?" asked Robinson suspiciously. They were not normally friends: Robinson was tall and nearly had a moustache. And he smoked.

"Got any matches? Or a lighter?" Ben asked without preamble.

"You started smoking, little Patty-boy? Or you gonna burn the school down?" He laughed at his own wit.

"Burn the school down, of course," Ben replied.

To his amazement Robinson handed over a book of matches. "From a sex bar in town – my brother got them. Don't show anyone the picture!"

Ben looked, and saw a minute photo of a couple in an unlikely embrace. He shrugged. "Seen it on the internet," he said, pretending to yawn.

Robinson grabbed at the match book, but Ben was faster, and ran to stand outside the staffroom.

"I'll get you, Patty-thief – you wait!" called Robinson.

"Not if I see you first!" Ben called back.

"Yes, and what can I do for you?" asked a master on his way in.

"Oh – er – it's okay, sir, thank you," Ben faltered. "I'm just going to…" and he melted away.

He spent the rest of the day trying to avoid Robinson, and wondering how to put his sketchy plan into action. Kitchens were the obvious place for a fire to start, but he couldn't get in daylight without being seen. Or the science block – plenty of stuff to burn there – but labs were always kept locked between lessons. But the attics…! If he could get up there, he could make a small fire and be out in moments. And an attic fire wouldn't hurt the rest of the school.

Last lesson of the day was English. Half-way through "The Lady of Shallot," Ben raised his hand. "Please may I be excused, Sir? I'm not feeling very well."

The master looked at him with distaste. "Take yourself off to Matron, Patterson – and don't come back until she's given you the all-clear."

"Patty's got the lurgy!" he heard whispered round the class as he hastened out.

The corridors were empty. Occasionally a door slammed; voices recited, sang, or called out answers. Ben walked purposefully, branched left towards the lavatories, then took the next staircase upwards. And another, until he had reached the top floor.

He pushed open a low door to the roof space. There were the piles of old furniture and textbooks. A few pigeon feathers rose and sank in the draught from the open door. Where would be the best place, where would be logical? Many of the old books had fallen from their tidy piles, and lay spread-eagled on the dusty floor. As he turned, he knocked over a stack of yellowing photographs in wooden frames. Glass broke. He gathered some of the books, tearing up pages into tiny mouse-nest pieces, then arranged a few of the split wooden frames over the pile, as if they had just fallen there, and placed a couple of bits of broken glass across the top. A bonfire, but not too arranged-looking, he hoped.

He lit the paper. It flared up so quickly that he tore up more pages to feed it. He added more wood from the frames, snapping them against his shoe like twigs. He became engrossed in encouraging and tending the flames, helping breathe and grow. It was only when they started to lick along the floorboards that he remembered what he was supposed to be doing. He rushed out of the room, leaving the door wide open, and ran back down the stairs, slowing only when he reached the main corridor.

English was long over, and Ben joined the gaggle of boys making their way to the refectory for tea. Ben was not very hungry, and gave his sausages and most of his beans to his neighbours on either side.

"You still not well?" asked Johnson kindly. He and Ben had been friends since the first year, and Ben felt bad about deceiving him.

"I'm okay – it's just…"

The fire alarm went off.

They were well-drilled. There was immediate silence. They got into lines at the refectory doors. "This is not a practice! Keep to the left!" masters were calling. "Lead on!" One orderly line met another, all making for the nearest exit, until everyone was in the main courtyard, organised in their year groups – even the august sixth formers. Masters walked up and down the rows, checking boys against the registers. The Headmaster viewed from the steps.

Ben sneaked a glance upwards. Little plumes of smoke were floating from between the roof tiles; behind a dormer window flames pushed and played, until the glass gave way and a jet of fire swept hungrily outwards. There was a gasp of horror mixed with excitement from the crowd in the courtyard. This was real drama; you could see it, and smell it, and hear the flames begin to roar just as the fire engines sped into the school grounds. The Head signalled to the staff, and the boys were waved back, away from the school buildings, to the edge of the yard.

Ben saw his chance, and in the noise and confusion sidled away to the tennis courts. He found the chosen tree, and clambered out along its branch. He dropped into a sort of passage behind the gardens that the bin men used, out of sight of householders and school.

5

He walked home in a daze. How clever was that! And everyone was safe! He had a fleeting image of the secret sick bay… but nurses and patients would be the first to be rescued, surely. He shook the thought away.

He let himself in to the strange emptiness of his house, unlocking every room, switching the lights on and off as he went. Just checking. He had never been alone in it before. They had always had babysitters. "It's just for Kate," his mother had said. "I don't know why we bother," his father had said. "They'll be fine." And his mother had shushed him with a look. But now, no one would come in late, banging the front door a bit too loudly, and stamp upstairs; no one would tiptoe into his room, smoothing his hair and pulling the duvet straight. No sound of Kate waking for a moment and being persuaded to stay in her own room.

He was in his own bed. He thought back to the weeks in school, where you were watched all the time, even at night, surrounded by other boys snoring and sometimes crying. And the soft tread of the patrolling master's feet.

It was good to be in bed in his own home again. He would stay here for a while, sort himself out a bit, try contacting his dad, and then, Wales… He fell asleep imagining how pleased they would be to see him, and how proud of him they'd be…

He was woken next morning by loud banging on the door. His bedside clock said ten past eleven. The banging went on. He lurched round his room, looking for clothes. Oh, fuck, fuck, fuck – his stupid mother seemed to have packed everything! Then in a bottom drawer he unearthed some baggy and discarded pants, a t-shirt someone had brought him from Miami, and an old pair of jeans.

The banging went on. And the letterbox was flapped.

Well, he can just bloody wait till I'm bloody dressed, Ben thought, terrified that someone from school had come to take him back.

He thumped downstairs, opened the door a crack, and nearly laughed. It was Rodney from next door. Ben pulled the door wider, and Rodney pushed his way in, gazing suspiciously round the hall.

"Well, you gave us a fright, and no mistake. Saw the lights going on and off last night – thought I'd better call round to check everything was hunky-dory. Thought your mum and the little girl had come back." He paused, waiting for Ben to tell him something.

"Oh… no," Ben mumbled vaguely. "Er… they're still…"

"And how are your grandparents?"

"Fine…fine. In fact, I'm going over to theirs' soon," said Ben, suddenly understanding. "Just came back to pick up a few things." Which was true, in a way.

"No school, then?" asked Rodney, suspicious again.

"Inset day," said Ben firmly, and Rodney, beaten, backed out, full of promises to keep an eye on the property and keep in touch.

Ben slammed the door. The house had lost its promise of security. Was it better to pretend it was empty? – except that now Rodney knew it wasn't. Get on with the plan and get out, Ben thought, and went to the kitchen and started to hunt for food.

Nothing in fridge or freezer.

Nothing in the larder.

He got a chair, and peered into the built-in cupboards over the cooker and sink. Bingo!

He found a tin of Spam and a tin of processed peas. And one of mixed vegetables. And a tin of butter beans. Probably bought by Nan. He dropped the tins into the sink below.

In the next cupboard he found a half-used bag of polenta and some whole-wheat spaghetti, and some Vietnamese rice noodles. That was mum, in experimental mood.

He read the labels. The noodles were very quick to cook. He boiled the kettle according to the instructions and then set about opening the tin of Spam. His hand went out automatically to the hook where the tin-opener was kept, and found nothing. For fuck's sake – had she taken all the kitchen stuff, too? He kicked the chair hard in fury, then rummaged through the kitchen drawers. Ah – there was an opener – a manky iron bull's head one, but it would do. He opened the mixed vegetables and tipped them, unheated, into the bowl of noodles. Then he chopped up half the Spam, and added that. It looked rather good, like a photograph of foreign food in an old cookery book of Gran's.

He ate until the bowl was empty. He drank tap-water, and then felt so sleepy that he went to lie on the sofa in the sitting-room. He flicked on the television, left it on for company, and slept.

What had woken him?

Then he heard it again – a quiet scraping sound, as though a key were being turned in the lock.

Rodney again. But Rodney would have made more noise, surely? He knew Ben was in the house. The television was still on, so any one outside would assume there was someone in. Why hadn't they knocked, or rung the doorbell?

The scraping was coming from the back door, as well as the front. Two people?

Ben crept to the window. He peered out, trying not to disturb the lace curtain. The porch hid anyone at the front door, but there was a long low black car outside the house. It wasn't the sort of vehicle that friends came in. Ben was shaking. If they got in, where was he to go?

He thought of all the hiding places he had used when he was younger – all far too obvious. Front and back doors had stained glass, so he could be seen if he crossed the hall. Cupboards in the sitting-room were too small, and he knew the windows locked with a complicated key, kept in the desk.

The back door shook violently and began to crack.

Dazed with terror, Ben dived under the sofa, scraping his way past the sagging springs until he was out of sight. He lay uncomfortably still, hoping he was hidden, his face crushed into the carpet.

He heard the back door give way.

"It's all right – I'm in now," a voice shouted up the hallway.

Ben heard the man inside opening the front door for his partner.

"They've got those special locks," said the first man. "No opening those with credit cards," and he laughed.

"Come on then – let's find the little bugger!" said the second man. The voices were muffled, as if they were wearing masks.

Ben listened to feet clumping round the ground floor, opening and slamming doors and cupboards. He was barely breathing by the time they got to the sitting-room.

"Oh, very nice," sneered one of the men. "Let's have a bit of a sit down and watch the telly."

"Bugger all on, nowadays," said the other.

They thudded upstairs.

Ben didn't dare to move. More doors and drawers opened and slammed, hangers clattered out of wardrobes.

The men came downstairs to the kitchen.

"Someone's been here, though – food on the table, see? And the telly on."

Ben could have kicked himself, if he'd had room.

"The old guy was quite certain he was here – said he'd spoken to him. Going to his grandparents, he'd said. Which is funny, because I know for a fact that they're dead – I looked them up."

"Well, he hasn't had time to get far. Perhaps he's gone down the pub!"

There was a muffled silence for a few minutes, then the sound of footsteps and the front door opening and laughter as they banged it shut.

As the purr of the big engine faded, Ben eased himself from under the sofa, stretching painfully and taking great gulps of air. Were his grandparents really dead? He felt tears coming, but brushed them away – later. He had half expected someone from school to come looking for him, but that bastard Rodney had actually reported him to the Cleaners! "Catch the Carriers" was their slogan, and Rodney had helped them.

How could he prove he wasn't a Carrier? He must go before anyone else came hunting.

He went to his bedroom and sorted through what remained of his clothing – another baggy pair of jeans his mother knew he didn't like, a thick fisherman's sweater that Nan had knitted that had been too itchy to wear, and more old t-shirts, socks and pants. Then at the back of his cupboard he found an anorak that he'd disdained because it came from a supermarket. Useful now, he thought. Now, a bag. His parents had only heavy matching suitcases. Whatever had his mother used? He noticed the end of a roll of bin bags on the bed. But he couldn't carry… An idea occurred.

He came down from the attic carrying Great-uncle Jim's army rucksack. It was dusty and stiff, but usable. He rolled up his clothes and stuffed them in. There was plenty of room, and the webbing straps were still strong.

Food. He went back to the kitchen. Tins were heavy, but he had no choice. And the tin-opener – a weapon when tins were gone. What else? He thought furiously. Oh, maps! He knew the way by car, but he could hardly walk down the middle of the motorway… In the sitting-room he found an old AA book which fitted neatly into the front pocket.

Now what? His mind was buzzing but not settling anywhere. He pictured himself walking away, rucksack on his back, anorak tied round him… Boots! Where were his walking boots? Would they still fit? He rushed up to his room and rummaged. No boots anywhere, nor trainers – his stupid mother had obviously packed them. Fuck, fuck, fuck!

Then he had an idea, and went to his parents' bedroom. There was his mum's lacy underwear scrunched on the floor, and her best high heels; his dad's dressing-gown and dinner jacket lay incongruously together, while his collection of silk ties snaked across the carpet. He spotted his dad's walking boots, pristine in their original box. They were too big, so he pulled on a pair of his dad's thick socks – better! He searched for more thick socks to take with him.

Money. Even if he was walking he would need money. He clomped back to his bedroom. There was a small hole in his mattress where he kept his secret supply of sweets, chewing-gum, and money. Was it still there? His fingers groped inside. He felt the hardness of coins, and extracted several fifty-pence pieces, some pound and two-pound coins, and some paper. He had two twenty pound notes! He tucked his spoils into his jeans' pocket.

Looking up, he saw the light was fading. Oh god, oh god, he must go! The Cleaners were devious; they would wait until he felt safe again, then pounce. He hurtled downstairs with the rucksack, stopping only to grab the remains of the Spam and cram it and his anorak into…

He heard the low rumble of a large car and froze.

He should have left sooner.

The engine stopped, and he heard the doors slam.

"Better put the suits on," said one of the men. "And the masks. He's bound to have crawled out from wherever he was by now."

The gate clanged. Ben raced to get out into the garden. As he tugged the damaged back door open, he heard the men crash the front door wide. He sidled along the wall of the house, and following the fence to the bottom of the garden where there was a gap, he squeezed through, shrugging away the brambles. He turned for a final look at his home. Lights were on in every room. He could hear the banging of doors and see the men's shadows against the windowpanes.

He was out in the road that ran parallel to his own. There were no street lights yet, so the Cleaners would not see him. He paused for a moment, wondering what was best to do.

He must start walking to West London for the motorway. They'd always driven that way; he knew the journey well. Then it dawned on him: he must have enough money to go by train – quicker, and probably safer than walking the streets.

The local station was nearby. It was quiet. He went over to the dim glow of the ticket office.

"Yes?" snapped a voice, as he peered at the window.

"Single to…" and Ben paused. How far could he go? "Chiswick?" Ben asked. He remembered that was near the motorway.

"Travelling alone?" asked the voice.

Oh god! thought Ben – he's going to check up on me and tell the Cleaners.

"Yea," mumbled Ben. "Going back to my Mum's – been staying with my Dad."

He was surprised at how easy he found it to lie. It was a good lie, too, implying that he was from a broken home

– a poor little waif pushed from one parent to the other.

The voice was not impressed. The ticket was slapped down, and a large quantity of Ben's money taken. "PlatformatformthreechangeatClaphamJunction. Threeminutes. Nomoretrainswhenyoureachthelimit," he was told.

What limit? Ben wondered, and he thudded down the stairs to the platform as the train drew in.

He dropped his rucksack on the seat beside him and looked round. Of the few people travelling, he seemed to be the youngest. He wished he were taller and older-looking. But at least he was on his way.

He changed at Clapham Junction, and no one took any notice of him as he wandered about looking for his next train. He settled on the carriage's dusty seat, leaning against his rucksack for comfort and safety, watching the suburbs rattle by. Not many houses with lights on, and the side streets were deserted. No buses and few cars, but there were lorries and vans, and the usual police cars and ambulances screaming about. Perhaps everyone had left already, Or perhaps there were just very few people left.

6

The house was theirs now. Its grey stone, layered with slate so it looked striped, the stained-glass window over the front door, the garden that lay up steps to the side of the house, with its lavender and roses and thick field grass – it was all so familiar that all thought of the London house was fading.

But the village wasn't theirs, yet. No one knocked at the door, or waved to them when they were in the garden. Mrs. Phillips in the house behind kept away from her windows; Mrs. Squibbs on the other side of the lane scurried inside if she saw Liz. She never saw the milkman: he left a bill tucked in an empty bottle and she wrote him a cheque.

They were beginning to run out of things – they'd used most of the frozen meat and vegetables she'd brought, and it seemed silly to start on the tins when there was a shop in the village. Loo roll. And coffee. Maybe some nice biscuits for Kate who professed to despise her mother's home-made ones. She just needed the courage to go. There were two small supermarkets in Cardigan twenty minutes away by car, but she was reluctant to waste petrol.

She took the backpack from its place behind the front door. "We're going shopping, Kate – come on!"

"No car?" said Kate.

"No, we're only going to the village shop – we can walk. I tell you what, you bring your rucksack, too, then perhaps we can find some treats."

They went along the narrow path that ran behind the cottages opposite. The children called it the "secret path". On one side was the broad sweep of the river, on the other, little waterfalls and rivulets ran from the ends of people's gardens. It was a point of pride to negotiate this walk without getting wet feet. Liz, in sandals, didn't much care, but Kate in trainers ran ahead, jumping and leaping, trying not to splash, and looking round for approval. She was probably missing school. Another thing to think about.

The path opened on to the High Street facing "Creepy Cyril's". Cyril stood at the door, scanning for customers. He was a tall, stooped man with red ears. It was said the shop could never keep a girl assistant long because of his hands, which were at the moment in his pockets.

"Back again?" he said. "Not holidays again, is it?"

"Can't keep away," said Liz, smiling politely.

"Looking for something in particular?" he asked. He didn't move.

Liz walked purposefully towards him, Kate shadowing her. "We've come to do some shopping," she said when they were face to face.

He leapt back into the shop. Liz took a wire basket and started hurling things in before he could object. Kate followed with her own basket.

Cyril muttered something in Welsh.

"What's that?" said Liz, turning to face him. "This is a shop, isn't it? And you are open?"

Cyril, torn between fear and greed, said, "You can't be too careful nowadays. People coming down from London, like, bringing Lord knows what with them…" He paused.

"If you mean the disease, we've been down here for weeks and we're still alive!" she said.

"Bethan? Bethan!" Cyril called, eyes fixed on Liz. His wife bustled forward.

"Hello, Bethan – how are you?" Liz asked.

"Well, at the moment," Bethan said. "You going to sell to them, or what?" she said to her husband, "I mean, she's got a point – they've been down here quite a while now…"

"And we're fine. So if you'd let us get on with our shopping…?" Liz ventured further into the shop, Kate at her side. "Now," she said, "we can have chops if you like – but they're not as good as the ones from the butcher in town – what do you think?"

"Sausages," said Kate firmly. "And oven chips and frozen peas."

Liz laughed. "Just this once," she said. "And we need vegetables, and loo roll, and coffee…"

"Boring," said Kate. "Let's get some crisps, and two

of those cakes with icing and custard in the middle – we can have a feast!"

"All right, then. Perhaps I'll get a bottle of wine, too…"

"If you're having wine, I want Tizer!" declared Kate.

At the checkout, Cyril was wearing a pair of out-sized rubber gloves.

"We aren't ill, are we? " Kate asked as soon as they were out of the shop.

"No, of course we're not," said Liz.

"Then why are they so mean?"

"They're frightened," answered Liz. "Like Ben's schoolmaster."

Kate nodded. "When they know us better, they won't mind us so much."

Cyril had known Liz most of her life and had been at school with her father. "The one that got away," was how Cyril had referred to Tom Lloyd Jones, a glint of jealousy in his eye.

"We'll manage," said Liz, grasping Kate's hand.

"The three of us," said Kate.

Light seeped round the edge of the curtains. Liz wondered for a moment where she was, then all the worries poured back. Ben. Kate's schooling. Money. The London house. Michael – was he really too busy to contact them? Surely even in his important work, he could take a moment to talk to them? And Ben. Her head hurt; she had drunk most of the bottle of wine… it would be so easy to do that every night. And Kate hadn't eaten very much of the food she'd chosen…

The curtain billowed and she caught a whiff of clean sea air. She dozed. She heard seagulls screech, scream, cry.

The sound was in the house – Kate!

She ran to look on Kate's restless form. The duvet was on the floor; Kate's face was flushed and damp.

"Mum," Kate said, keeping her eyes closed, "Mum, my head hurts – I'm hot…" She pulled her pyjama jacket over her face. "It's too light."

Liz felt her forehead. "Just a moment," said Liz. "We'll soon make you feel better – I'll be right back."

She rummaged around in the bathroom cabinet for the Calpol – found a plastic measuring spoon that her mother must have kept there. She wrung out a flannel under the cold tap, and went back to Kate. "Here we are," said Liz, scooping Kate into a sitting position to take the medicine. "This will help the headache, and this – " she spread the cold flannel over Kate's forehead – "will help to cool you down." She turned Kate to one side while she pulled the bottom sheet smooth and plumped up the pillow. "See if you can sleep again."

Kate was already asleep, breathing heavily.

Liz found some aspirin and went downstairs to make tea. She felt hollow with anxiety. Kate hadn't been in contact with her grandparents – could Liz have passed it on? Or at school…? Surely they would have been informed and the school closed, like Ben's. Not that she'd been told about that.

She scraped her chair back, and went to switch

the radio on for the first time since they'd arrived. She twisted the knobs, changing bands and stations until she found a news programme that wasn't in Welsh. The headlines were unchanging: – "…no need for panic… travel not recommended…" She knew all that – why do they keep repeating the same things? "… doctors or hospitals." Oh, god, what had she missed? She tried to concentrate. "… at home… and make all contacts by phone where possible. I repeat… the public is asked to refrain from using vital medical services."

Liz snapped the radio off. What were people supposed to do – just sit at home until they died? Yes, that was exactly what was expected. So there was no longer any routine medical service; hospitals were overwhelmed by the numbers of sick and dying, of the public and medical staff alike. All those sirens they had heard in London signalled people being rushed to intensive care units. A silent ambulance, she realised, was probably on its way to the mortuary.

What could she do about Kate? Suppose she, too, had developed the virus? They'd been breathing on each other, kissing goodnight, and hugging. How could she be sure without a doctor? Suppose Ben arrived and they were both – she said the word over and over again until it sounded nonsense. Dead dead dead. And if Kate's illness were that very thing that she'd fled to Wales to escape, what would Ben do? Never mind the infection – it would be better to be all together, no matter what.

Kate's voice, whining from upstairs, broke in.

"Mummy, Mummy, I want a drink of water."

Liz ran the tap until the water was cold, and carried the glass upstairs. Kate was flushed, and she whimpered when she tried to sit up. "My neck's all stiff."

Liz plumped up the pillows and helped Kate into a sitting position. Kate gulped the water. Her neck glands were swollen. Liz's hands shook as she took the glass.

"Don't like Welsh water," Kate said grumpily. "It tastes of swimming pool. Why can't I have proper water, out of a bottle, like we used to?"

"Sorry," said Liz. "You can't often find it now, and it's very expensive."

"Daddy would buy it – he's got lots of money."

"Well, he isn't bloody here, is he!" She was doing her best – they were in Wales where they were supposed to be safe, they had shelter, and they still had food and water. Kate began to weep into the duvet, and Liz was stricken with shame. "Never mind, poor baby, never mind, my love," she murmured, rocking the child in her arms.

"Everyone's gone," Kate snuffled. "And they didn't say goodbye."

"I know, I know," said Liz. "But Nan and Grampa would have been so pleased that we're in their house…"

"And daddy?" Kate asked with a sob.

"I don't know," said Liz, sniffing. Kate was crying anyway; there didn't seem much point in lying. "He went to stay in his office so that we wouldn't get infected. And his job is very important… He said he'd help us…"

"Is he all right?" Kate murmured.

"I don't know, my love," said Liz. "And I don't know where Ben is at the moment. I'm sure he's on his way."

Kate's blotchy face appeared from the duvet. "Three's nice," she said. "Can I have more Calpol? And can I sleep in your bed?"

In her own room, Liz straightened her bed and opened the window so she could breathe the green river smell overlaid by the sea's salty breeze. Fields patterned the river's far bank; a crest of trees stood against the thin pale sky. It was a tranquil scene.

She lifted Kate on to her tidied bed, and propped her against the pillows. One more dose of Calpol.

"There," said Liz. "You can see the river from here, and a little bit of the road. Can you smell the sea?"

"No," sliding further down the bed. "Can we go to the beach when Ben comes?"

"Of course we can! But we'll probably have to walk, you know. But it'll be lovely – we can take our costumes."

"Did you pack mine?"

"Yes. And we'll take a picnic, and stay as long as we like. And we can make a camp in the dunes, and maybe cook sausages over a fire like we did with Gramps, and we can swim, and find shells…"

They both slept.

7

Someone was shaking him. Ben pulled away in fright. A station guard looked at him angrily. Still dazed from sleep, Ben didn't understand what the man wanted.

"… bed here for the night!" he was saying threateningly. "You've come to the end! And I'll bet you haven't got a ticket!"

Now Ben understood, he produced his ticket from his anorak pocket with a flourish.

"Right, well, you can't go no further. And where are you off to, anyway, at this time of night? The Cleaners'll get you, out by yourself." He hesitated. "You're not a Runner, are you? You can't go wandering round the country nowadays, not with things the way they are…"

"I'm meeting my Dad," Ben said quickly. "I've just been staying with my Mum, and now I'm going to his…" He could hear how pathetic he sounded; there was even a hint of tears in his voice which was not entirely acting.

The guard gave him a long look. "Off the train, then, and out of my sight, or I'll have to report you! Go on, now – skedaddle!"

Ben hitched his rucksack on, jumped out of the carriage and scuttled into the station waiting-room in case the guard was watching him. From the window he saw the train disappear into a tunnel. Ben would like to have stayed in the station for a while, perhaps to sleep. It was a pleasant building, like a little house, with a wooden canopy. But he had to leave. There were now two people who had seen him go – the guy in the ticket office, and now this guard.

He started walking. Right, he thought. That was the way the train had gone, so left would take him back towards London. The road curved round along an unlit street of tidy houses. Even in the dark he could see that these were homes his mum would have called "posh", in that slightly disapproving way of hers. He picked up his pace, trying not to dwell on the reasons for the absence of light and people. The more he tried not to think, the wilder his imagination became. He wished he had never watched horror videos.

Then the houses were replaced by glassy dark office blocks, set back from the road.

Where am I now? he wondered. He wished he'd brought the old A to Z from the bookcase in the sitting-room, and the ordnance survey maps for Wales, which he loved so much more than the boring cold directions on his smart phone. Not that his phone was working any more.

Then he came to a high brick wall surrounding a courtyard full of light and noise. Men were loading lorries, carrying large boxes and metal barrels – it was the brewery they'd always passed on the way to Wales. He remembered his father saying that Fuller's Ale was sold all round the country... Ben sidled into the courtyard in the shadow of the wall.

The loaders and drivers were calling to each other – "Can you fit another barrel in there? Governor'll kill us if we don't travel full", and "Anyone going West? 'Cos you could drop off a parcel for the wife, if you made a stop before the bridge..."

"I'll do it," called one of the men, "but it'll cost you...!"

"Buy you a pint, then," said the first.

"Whisky, more like!"

Ben held his breath. "West" and "Bridge" meant the lorry was going towards Wales.

He slid out of the shadows towards a stack of unpacked boxes, and crouched down. "Fuller's Ales" was printed on the sides, and "Feel fitter with Fuller's!" printed in curly mock-Victorian script.

Ben worked his way across the yard, stopping to hide behind a box or barrel as he went, until he was close to the lorry he hoped was going to Wales. Now what? He watched. The loaders seemed to have stopped, though the lorry was not yet full – yes, Ben could see them, having a cigarette by the cab. Before they could return to work, Ben scurried to the back and hoisted himself in, feeling his way between the stacks of boxes and barrels until he found a big enough space. He squeezed in, pulling his rucksack after him. He could see light through the gaps, and hoped the dark interior would camouflage him.

More shouting and thudding and the load was completed; there was a crash as the shutter descended.

The engine started and they were off – the driver, the beer, and Ben.

He punched the air in delight – hardly any walking, and he was on his way! Not that he minded walking, but this was so much quicker. At this rate he'd be in Wales in – well, in no time!

Now there was nothing to look at he felt suddenly hungry. He reached into the rucksack and ate some of the leftover Spam. But he was thirsty – fancy not bringing water – how stupid! Then he had an idea, and groped for the tin opener.

He slit open the edge of the nearest box. Rows and rows of cans. He pulled one out and opened it. He'd drunk lager before, but this was different: dark and almost sweet, with a bitter aftertaste. He wasn't sure that he really liked it, but it quenched his thirst. He glugged happily.

Suddenly he was sleepy. He fidgeted about trying to get comfortable, wedging himself against a keg with his rucksack as a pillow, trying to keep his spinning head still. Woozily he tried to plan what to do when the lorry arrived – how would he know where he was? How would he get out without being seen?

His eyes closed, and he drifted off to sleep.

There was loud rattling, and his head hurt. He could hear voices outside, coming from the driver's cabin. A woman was asking about her parcel. "He told me he'd send it me, along with you-know-what. That it, then? Mind how you handle it – belonged to my mam, that clock did..." The voices faded for a moment. Ben imagined them walking round to unlock the back of the lorry.

Then he heard, "Any chance of some breakfast then? Or shall we sort things out first?"

"Come and eat, why don't you? Then we can see about shifting some of this stuff." The shutter stayed locked as the footsteps died away.

How was he to get out? It was daylight now; he could see light from a slit of a window at the back of the driver's cabin. He began to work his way towards the shutter. There was little room to move. He advanced by pushing a box into the space he had just vacated, risking toppling the cargo and making a racket. He edged on, until he heard voices again. Breakfast must be over. He had a sudden yearning for bacon and eggs.

"So...?" said the woman.

"Right you are," the man replied. "How much do you want to take this time?" He unlocked the back, and daylight poured through gaps in the cargo. Ben ducked and hid his face.

"Well, I can get rid of a couple of barrels, and maybe four boxes – what do you think?"

"You can have it if you can pay for it, you know

that, and as long as it doesn't make too big a hole in the load…"

"Perhaps I'll take another couple of boxes?"

"Okey-dokey – suits me." The man strained and huffed as he hefted out the boxes and barrels. Fingers of light pointed into the lorry. Ben stayed rigid.

"Right – that's you sorted," said the man.

"Well, come back to the café and I'll pay you out of the till – don't suppose you do cheques, eh?"

To Ben's relief, the shutter remained unlocked. The footsteps died away, and he shoved his way out, dragging his rucksack. He jumped down off the tailgate and ran to the shelter of some nearby trees and bushes. He looked round.

The lorry, a few others, and four or five cars stood in a service-station car park. He didn't recognise it, and couldn't make out the name. It was not one they had stopped at as a family; their first break had always been just before the Bridge. Where was he? Of course, he could go and find out: no one had seen him arrive, he was hungry, and his head still ached. He checked his pocket for cash and reckoned he had more than enough for an all-day breakfast. He shouldered the rucksack, emerged from the bushes, and strode across the tarmac in full view to the front of the café, and nearly shouted with relief. He was in Wales! At Magor – yes, he remembered seeing the name on previous journeys. The lorry had probably crossed the Bridge earlier that morning.

He walked over to the woman behind the counter.

"Can I have the all-day breakfast, please?" he asked.

"You'd have to wait all day if that's what you want," said the woman. "I got eggs and bread and no more food coming in today."

"That's fine," said Ben. He knew her voice – the driver had sold the beer to her.

She turned round to start frying eggs and butter some thin white bread. "Come far, have you? Only it's not good times to be wandering about on your own," and she cast a glance at his rucksack.

"Oh, I'm meeting my dad soon." Ben hoped the story would work again.

The woman said nothing; she dished up his eggs and bread, and gave him an unasked-for cup of tea. Ben paid and went to sit down – there were plenty of tables. He ate, glad to be anonymous.

He scanned the few travellers and wondered who might make a credible father. All he had to do was finish his food and walk out confidently as if they were meeting in the car park. Easy.

The woman waylaid him as he got up to go, ambling towards him, swishing a dishcloth over tables. "You sure you're being met? We don't need Runners carrying germs and stuff into our nice clean country… know what I mean?" She kept her voice low and her distance from Ben.

"Outside," Ben faltered. "I'm meeting him outside, in the car park…"

"Because he wouldn't sit with me inside! Moody, eh?" came a voice behind Ben. "You know what young lads are like, eh? Come on, now, my boy…" and the man dug his fingers hard into Ben's shoulder and marched him out of the door.

"But you're not – he's not – no, no – let go of me!" Ben stuttered and struggled, kicking and squirming, but the man's grip was a vice, and he held Ben's arm in a half nelson.

"Oh, well, if he's yours, then," the woman was saying, carefully not watching, and happy to be rid of the problem. Ben, wriggling and ducking, was led across the car park to a dark blue Mercedes, and shoved onto the front seat.

"There you are, boy," said the man. "Sorry to grab you like that, but needs must – got you safe away from her, didn't I?"

"Yes, but…" Ben began.

"Well, I knew you were telling fairy tales. You're a Runner, aren't you, eh? And you need a lift. And here am I, just at the right time, eh?"

"No!" Ben shouted. "I'm meeting my dad!" He fumbled with the car door. It was locked. Ben felt sick. He must get away. Better the woman in the café than this stranger. All the warnings Ben had ever heard from school and his parents poured into his terrified mind, as the man calmly turned on the ignition, and pulled out of the service station.

"Where shall we go, then?" the man asked.

Ben didn't reply.

"Oh, come on, now – we might as well be pleasant to each other. I'm Robert, by the way. I'm a Government Authorised travelling salesman, so I can go pretty much anywhere. You need it – I can get it for you." He grinned unpleasantly.

"Why aren't you afraid I'm a Carrier? I might infect you," Ben said.

Robert shot him a sideways look. "Well, sometimes you just have to take a bit of a risk, eh? And where would you be now, if I hadn't picked you up? Safe with the Cleaners, that's where. 'Oh, thank you, Rob – you saved me, Rob – I'll do anything you say, Rob,'" he added in a strange high-pitched voice that came oddly from his moist red lips.

Ben shuddered. "I'm going to Carmarthen," he said. Not too much risk there. He was actually aiming for Cardigan.

"Well, isn't that lucky, because that's exactly the way I'm going. That where your dad lives, then? Or your mum?" he said. "You're a wise one – play your cards close to your chest, eh?" He chuckled.

Ben clutched his rucksack tighter. The man drove fast and smoothly. Ben kept his face to the window, knowing the man wouldn't miss a single movement. They had passed signs to Cardiff and were now heading for Swansea. Ben began to recognise the roads. He had to get out.

There was a sign for a service station. "I need the toilet," Ben said.

"Oh, yes?" said the man. "Took you a good while to think up that one, eh?"

"But I do," Ben insisted. "Really badly. I might pee in your car…"

The man swore, and swerved off to follow the services sign. "Now, you listen to me, my boy," he said, when the car had slid to a halt. "There's to be no nonsense, see? No thinking you can slip away while my back's turned, because I shan't turn my back. And what will you do without me, anyway? The Cleaners are everywhere – they'll get you in the end!" He thrust his face towards Ben as he hissed this threat, and Ben recoiled from the heavy smell of aftershave and hair gel.

"I just need the loo," Ben said.

"Leave it!" snapped the man, as Ben went to pick up his rucksack. "You won't need that." As he let Ben out of the car, he grabbed his shoulder again, and swivelled him towards the toilets. "I'll be waiting for you."

There was no other way out, and Ben was forced to return to his captor, who greeted him cheerfully, buckling them both in and driving off. There was something about the way the man kept glancing at him that made Ben remember shocked conversations from school… Some of his classmates had had experiences, and narrow escapes. Now he had no idea how he could get away, and he groaned audibly in despair.

"Oh, we can't have that," said the man, with seeming

sincerity. "You got a problem, you tell me, eh? I saved you, didn't I? I'm your friend." To Ben's horror, the car slowed down and turned off the motorway.

"We'll just have a little rest, eh? And you can tell me what's bothering you." He brought the car to a stop in a lay-by in a narrow country lane. "Let's get comfy, then," and he turned to undo both their seat belts.

Ben tried to persuade himself that the man was harmless, wanted to be his friend, to help him get back to his family. Then he saw that look in his eyes – intent, pleading, cold – and the horrible red line of his lips. Ben groaned again, and was violently sick, over himself, Robert and the front of the car.

"Christ almighty!" shrieked the man. "Why the fuck didn't you tell me? It's not even my car!" He leapt out, retching, and went to the boot. "You stay there while I clean up, you little shit – don't you move!"

As soon as he was ransacking the boot for cleaning cloths, Ben was out and clutching his rucksack.

He dived through the hedge and ran.

For a while he heard the man raving and swearing. "I'll get you! I'll tell the Cleaners!" And then, wailing, "But we were friends! I was going to get you home…"

The voice retreated as Ben pounded on, the bag bumping on his back, down the edge of a field, under a sheltering hedgerow, and over a stile. He stumbled round the edges of two more fields before he felt safe enough to stop and catch his breath. He fell to the ground where he stopped, curling up with his head on his knees, panting and listening. There was silence now – no voice calling, no feet, and no car – and no road in sight. There was only the sound of small hedge-hopping birds, and the faint breeze riffling the leaves. He smelt the sweetness of the earth and grass, and breathed in deeply, wanting to feel the clean air inside him. He became aware of a terrible stink; he'd been sick over one sleeve and his anorak. Water. He needed to wash and drink and think. Then somewhere safe to rest, to study the map and find out where he was.

8

Liz was woken by an insistent tapping at the front door. Whatever was the time? She saw it was afternoon, and rose from the bed. Kate woke briefly, then her eyelids rolled shut again.

The tapping persisted. Ben, she thought immediately. But why hadn't he come in round the back? Maybe he wanted to surprise them. Liz rushed downstairs and flung open the door.

"Mrs. Phillips!" she exclaimed. It was impossible to keep the disappointment out of her voice. Mrs Phillips was the neighbour whose garden backed on to their house, a widow who had always been polite, but never quite friendly. "Come in, come in," Liz said, trying to sound welcoming.

"I can see you didn't expect me," said Mrs. Phillips, walking straight in. "I've been waiting to see if your parents or your husband turned up, but you seem to be rather on your own. Tell me to bugger off and leave you alone – I'll quite understand," she added seeing Liz's eyes fill with tears. "And I hadn't seen the little girl about for a day or so, and I did wonder if everything was all right."

"You mean you wondered if she'd got the sickness," said Liz, "So you can tell the village and get us out of here!" To her shame, she started sobbing. She wanted to be angry, and throw the visitor out, but she couldn't stop weeping.

"So she is ill?" asked Mrs. Phillips.

Liz nodded. "But I'm sure she hasn't been in contact… And I don't know what's the matter, and you can't get a doctor any more…" Liz struggled.

"It's a bad time," Mrs. Phillips said. "Do you mind if I have a quick look? I used to be a nurse, and my husband was a doctor – I do have some idea of what's what."

"But what about infection?" Liz asked, surprised.

"Too old," was the reply. Mrs. Phillips led the way upstairs as if she knew her way round. "Used to visit you mother here, years ago, before they move to London. Lovely woman. Is she in here?" She paused at the door to the back bedroom.

"No – she's in here with me," said Liz, opening the door a crack and peering in. Kate lay on her front, with the covers kicked off and her pyjama top rucked up. Her back was sprinkled with small red dots.

"There you are, then," said Mrs. Phillips, pushing past her. "It is a virus, but not the virus. Chickenpox," she said succinctly. "Those spots will blister and scab. You mustn't let her scratch them, or she'll scar."

Liz flopped on the bed.

"What car?" said a sleepy voice.

"Mrs. Phillips says you've got chickenpox," said Liz.

"Can you die of chickenpox?" asked Kate.

"Not easily," said Mrs. Phillips.

"That's all right, then," Kate replied, and pulled her pyjama jacket down primly. "Can I have a story, mummy?"

"Just let me make Mrs. Phillips some tea, and I'll be up. Shut your eyes again."

Downstairs, Liz put the kettle on, and spooned tea into the pot. Her hands were shaking.

"You've still got proper tea, I see," said Mrs. Phillips. "Can't get it any more round here. Not that Cyril ever stocked anything decent."

Liz opened a cupboard and brought out her last treasured packet of Fortnum's Famous Breakfast Blend.

"Please," she said, "take this."

"No, no, no! I can't take that!"

"But I should really like you to have it, and I don't mind teabags – really. You don't know how much you've helped me," she went on clumsily. "I thought she was going to die…"

"Goodness! Well, I'll take it. And thank you. We'd better pour this – do you have milk?"

They took their mugs to the sitting-room and sat facing each other in silence for a while. Liz saw the weathered lines of the old woman's face, and her kind, pale eyes.

"Have you lost someone?" Liz said.

"Oh, at my age it happens all the time – not a week goes by but someone falls off the perch… Not children, though," she added hastily, seeing Liz's face. "We never did have children, Sam and I. And then Sam had a heart attack – years ago now. Nothing to do with this… What about you?" she asked abruptly.

"My mother, and then my father – he was the one who told us to get away…" Suddenly Liz found herself telling Mrs. Phillips about Ben, and how they were waiting for him. "And we've no idea if he got away from his school, or how he'll get here… or even if he's…" Liz's voice trailed away.

"I gather the father isn't about?" said Mrs. Phillips at last.

Liz shook her head. "He works all the time. You know – important Government stuff." She giggled feebly. "I think there's still money coming in, though, and then I need need to do something about the other house if I can… it's not safe to leave it empty, and I can't afford to run two houses in these days…"

Mrs. Phillips stood up to go. "You need to find out exactly what the situation is, you know."

"I've been putting it off," Liz admitted.

"Yes, well, nothing is going to get better, my dear. You must be prepared. You may have arrived well-stocked, but you must have noticed the shops aren't as full as they used to be. We're all going to have to be more self-sufficient – oh, don't look so distressed! People will get used to you in time, and you'll get some help! I can help you – I grow all my own vegetables, you know – cabbages, beetroot… But one word of advice, if you will allow me," Mrs. Phillips looked concerned. "If – when – your boy arrives, don't let the village know until you're absolutely sure…"

She saw Mrs. Phillips out, placing her hand gently on the older woman's shoulder. "Thank you," she said.

Days passed; Liz lost count. Kate scratched and wept and slept, and demanded stories. She ate nothing, then asked for exotic things like Nutella and peanut butter – "But not the gritty one, mummy."

"I don't know that Cyril stocks them, but I can go and see, if you like," Liz said.

"I don't want you to you go out and leave me," Kate moaned.

"Then you'll have to do without – unless you fancy walking with me."

Kate slid out of bed and pulled on her clothes. "I'll come," she said. The diet of milkman's eggs and bread and butter was beginning to pall.

Kate was tired after five minutes, dragging her feet.

"Look," said Liz reasonably, "either we walk together, or you go back home by yourself. Or," she added, suddenly inspired, "you can sit on this wall here and wait till I come back – it won't take long."

"All right," Kate agreed, "but will you bring me something nice even if they don't have Nutella?"

"I'll try."

Cyril and Bethan's shop had changed since their last visit. There was still food on the shelves, but only one tin or jar deep. The freezers were nearly empty, only some greying mince and chicken wings remained.

She looked along the preserves section, plum jam and finely shredded marmalade – no Nutella and no peanut butter.

"Can I help you?" asked Cyril.

"Oh, I was just looking for a treat for Kate… Nutella?" she asked.

He shook his head mournfully. "Can't get the supplies, now. Not enough petrol, not enough drivers – not enough people in the factories, either." A recital of doom. "Don't know what's going to happen to us, now – it's all going down the pan."

Liz shook her head in sympathy, and moved off round the shop again, torn between stocking up with anything that was there, and indulging Kate. There was little to tempt a sick child. On her second walk round she decided on the chicken wings, and a small jar of honey, some dying spring onions, papery garlic and an expensive bunch of carrots. She paid and hurried out of the shop.

Kate still perched on the wall, but she wasn't alone. Several children crowded in front of her, pointing but not touching. They didn't sound friendly. Liz walked faster. "Come on, Kate," Liz called brightly. "Let's go home and cook!"

"She yours?" asked a big skinny girl.

Liz nodded, and held out her hand to Kate.

"She got the plague, then?" said a small boy, eyes large with curiosity.

"Of course not!" Liz snapped.

"Then what's all them spots on her arm?" the small boy persisted.

Kate had been scratching. "It's chickenpox, and it's very catching," said Liz. "If you haven't had it, you need to keep away. Come on, Kate!"

The group sloped off, muttering "plague" and "virus" and "chicken pox". She hugged Kate, who was quietly crying. "You took so long."

"Well, I'm here now," Liz said. "Off we go – we're going to have a Chinese takeaway tonight!"

"Really?" asked Kate, brightening up.

"Well, we'll have to cook it," said Liz.

"But then it won't be a takeaway," Kate wailed.

On the way back, Liz explained how to do a homemade takeaway of fried rice and spiced chicken wings. Kate stopped complaining. "Ben will like that," she said.

"We'll do it again when he comes," Liz promised.

9

Kate was getting well again. They'd enjoyed their mock takeaway, and started making plans about what they'd do when Ben arrived: how they could make his room nice, what they could cook for him, and how they'd go to the beach together. Liz played the game well, though it took a huge effort not to keep saying, "perhaps", and "maybe", and "let's hope", and "if…"

Liz knew she must look at their finances. Her card still worked, but that could change at any moment – she had no idea what Michael had organised for them if he he'd had the time. Perhaps she had emptied the account already, spent everything. Maybe the banks themselves would stop functioning, as shops were beginning to – how would they manage then?

She had never had to bother about money since her marriage. She had paid the bills and bought the food from the joint bank account. She was a modest spender. Michael had teased her at first, and then was increasingly annoyed. "For god's sake, you don't have to go about looking like some superannuated hippy! Buy yourself something nice for once – get your hair done!"

By which he meant, of course, "make yourself look like the wives of the people I work with." She had preferred to rummage through charity shops for a "find" – a embroidered Indian coat, a silk-lined nineteen-forties jacket...

"... and then when we go to the beach... You're not listening, Mummy!" Kate spoke indignantly.

"Yes, yes, I am," Liz replied vaguely.

"So what did I just say, then?"

"You said – let's get the washing-up done and then have a story in bed!"

"No, I didn't," Kate giggled. "You're so silly, Mummy!"

"Well, tomorrow I've got to stop being silly and go to the bank. But now, you get ready for bed and choose a story, and I'll do the washing-up, okay?"

"Okay. But I don't want to go to the bank. And suppose Ben comes while we're out?"

"I should hope he'd have enough sense to wait for us!" Liz. "Anyway, you could write him a note."

Instead of going to bed, Kate found writing paper from the desk, and began laboriously to write a note for her brother. She showed it to Liz.

"Here, mummy, is this nice?"

Liz took the letter and smiled although she wanted to grab the medicinal brandy.

"Deer ben," Kate had written, "we have gon to the bnk and we wil be bak son. luv Kate and mum. ps plees wate for us."

Had Kate always written so badly? They hadn't

complained at school, but the teachers had had other worries. She must pay more attention to Kate's education. She was beginning to read, which was a good sign, but the nearest school was a Welsh Medium school, where everything was taught in Welsh, and that wouldn't begin until autumn. She'd have to nurse Kate through that when the time came. Meanwhile, she'd try to persuade Kate that English was not a phonetic language.

"Come on, Kate," Liz called up the stairs next morning. "Hair brush, tooth brush, pee!"

"But I'm not going to school, am I? I don't think I'm very well – I'm still too tired – I might get chicken pox again…"

"It's still summer holidays, and you need to be ready – we're going into town."

Drawers and doors banged upstairs.

"I want you to make me a list while you have breakfast," Liz said. "First, ask Mrs. Phillips about buses, and if she wants anything; second, go to the bank, and third, see what we can find for dinner. Oh, and before that, I'd like you to get the wheely bag out of the shed."

Kate stopped scratching with the pencil and ran out to the shed. Liz sneaked a look at the list: she had written "buss, miss p, wonts, bnk, din…" Still, it was rather clever to précis the list so neatly.

"What's next?" she asked as Kate came back with the trolley.

"Buses and Mrs. Phillips," she replied promptly.

"Right, well you go and ask…"

"But I don't know her. I don't want to ask – I'll forget!"

"I'll go to town by myself," Liz threatened.

Kate went off to knock very quietly on Mrs. Phillips's door, hoping she'd be out.

Liz was about to fetch her daughter when Kate reappeared, waving a long strip of paper. "There's a bus in half an hour, she says, but not one back until five o' clock, and this is a list of things she'd like but only if it's not too much trouble and not too heavy so I told her about the wheely bag…"

Liz laughed, and took the list from her. "Oh, you wrote the list for her?" she said in surprise.

"Yes, because she said it was good practice. And she helped me spell all the difficult words. Because no one else does," she add pointedly.

Kate spent the bus journey reading her list, while Liz worried about the bank, and wished she'd brought a book with her. Just turning the pages and scanning print was an act she found soothing. She tried to concentrate on breathing calmly instead, which didn't work.

"Why are you puffing, Mummy?" Kate asked.

Once they were at the bank she felt less inclined to worry. What had been an imposing Edwardian building was now badly in need of painting. The ATM was boarded up, the brass door fittings unpolished. There was only one cashier on duty.

Liz introduced herself, and at the sound of her name a door opened and the manager appeared.

"Gareth Morgan," he said, leading Liz to a chair in his office. "And this must be your little one," he added, as Kate followed closely. "Recognised the name. Knew you father years ago – a good man, he was. I trust…?" But Liz shook her head. She didn't want to go into family history just then. "How can I help?"

"It's about the state of my account. I mean, I haven't had time to sort things out since we arrived… and all the bank statements go to the London house…"

"Have we got any money left?" Kate chirped.

"First things first," said Mr. Morgan, and Liz felt he wanted to pat Kate and herself kindly on the head. "Have you some form of identification? Just a formality, of course – you have the look of your father about you."

Liz produced her passport, driving licence, and the deeds to the Welsh house which she'd discovered in the desk drawer, and waited while Mr. Morgan examined each document in slow detail.

"Well," he said finally, returning everything to Liz. "All in order, as I knew it would be. Now…" and he clicked swiftly through a screen full of numbers. "Let's see… What exactly did you want to know?"

"Am I spending too much – is there anything left?" She felt like Kate.

"There are the usual regular deposits. Nothing untoward."

"Could you be just a little more precise?" Liz asked.

Mr. Morgan handed her a printout of last three months' statements. All the usual direct debits were being taken, and, amazingly, Michael's salary continued to be paid in. So he was still alive and working? Or had no one noticed that he wasn't? Liz sighed. A tear slid down her cheek. Kate's arms went round her. "Don't cry, Mummy – I don't mind eating Mrs. Phillips' cabbages, really…"

"It's all okay, my love," said Liz. "You're saved from the cabbage diet for a while yet."

Mr. Morgan cleared his throat. "There, now. All is well. If you need any help…?" He paused. "A reinvestment of your account?"

Liz shook her head. "Thank you for your help, Mr. Morgan, but I don't think we'll bother you any more."

She and Kate left through the swing doors and into the High Street.

They toured the High Street for Mrs. Phillips' shopping, and managed to find her some loose tea and coffee beans, and the local cheese and bacon she wanted. Liz bought some, too.

"Can we afford that, mummy?" asked Kate sternly.

"You know what?" Liz said. "We can buy what we like today!" One spree would not hurt.

"Let's get a telly!" said Kate.

The electrical shop's windows were festooned with "Closing Down" notices and televisions were marked at less than half price.

"That's really cheap, isn't it?" Kate said longingly.

"Yes," said Liz, "But think why."

"Perhaps they don't work any more," Kate suggested sadly. "Like your laptop and your phone."

"Exactly," said Liz. "And do you remember how you got sick of the repeats when we were in London? No one's making programmes any more."

Kate sighed. "Can we go to the market?" That had always been a treat – stalls for food, clothes, books, sewing, wool, and Kate's favourite – jewellery and hair-slides of bright plastic and glass.

Again, Kate was disappointed. "There's nothing here!" she grumbled. "Only old junk."

She was right. No more craft stalls, with fabrics and knitting wool, no more shiny jewellery, and no more antiques and second-hand books. Instead, there were piles of old clothes, records, china, and pots and pans. People were obviously trying to make a bit of cash while they could. Kate tugged her hand impatiently, so they moved on to look at the food. At least that had not changed; there was still a good supply of local meat and vegetables and fish.

Liz bought home-cured ham, and sewin.

"I don't like fish!" Kate said.

"But this is very rare and delicious – and pink," Liz replied. She bought sausages, potatoes and onions, and a huge lettuce. "That should do us for a while," she said.

"I don't like lettuce." Kate was beginning to flag.

"Come on," said Liz. "Treats time!"

They crossed the road and went into the bookshop, where they each chose several books, and bought new felt tips, crayons and a pad of drawing paper for Kate. Liz bought two newspapers – not so much for news, but so she could attempt the crosswords.

Then they bought some welsh cakes, a loaf made of flour from the local mill, and some lamb from the butcher, who recognised her and asked kindly after Michael and Ben.

"Working," said Liz, and "At school." She paid quickly and left.

"That wasn't really true, was it?" said Kate, trying to catch up with Liz who was dragging the bag clumsily in the direction of the bus stop.

"Chops tonight!" said Liz, too brightly, as Kate caught up. Then stopped in the middle of the pavement.

"Is the bag too heavy now?" Kate asked. "I'll help you pull!"

Liz didn't move.

"Mummy! Mind! You're in the way!" She tried to lug the bag out of people's way.

Tears were running down Liz's cheeks and dripping off her chin.

"Don't – don't!" Kate began to cry. "Is it the bag, Mummy? Have we spent too much?" She clung round her mother's waist.

"All got a bit much for you?" a woman asked. Leaning into the nearby chemist's shop, she called, "Got a chair, Gwilym?"

Liz, with Kate still clinging to her, was ushered inside.

She sat down gratefully but couldn't speak. The tears

continued to pour and she breathed with difficulty. She clutched at Kate's hand. "Sorry," she tried to say. "Sorry. Better in a minute."

A cup of tea appeared from nowhere, and she slurped some of it down between gasps. There were murmurings in the background. The woman was talking to Kate, and Kate sounded sensible and grown-up. She took a few shuddering gulps of air, and looked round for somewhere to put the cup. "Okay now," she said. She felt bewildered and ashamed.

"Nothing like tea to pick you up. And here's your Kate all ready to look after you and by the time you're home you'll be a new woman, Mrs. Patterson!"

"How do you…?" Liz began in surprise.

"Live up the lane from your Mrs. Phillips – Mari Evans, I am. Knew your dad, too, when he was a boy. Now can you walk a bit? Nearly time for the bus."

Mari Evans helped Liz up, got hold of Kate and the bag, and was halfway out of the shop before Liz remembered to thank Gwilym the chemist.

Mrs. Evans kept up a stream of chatter all the way back – "Always fond of your dad, I was…That Mrs. Phillips… heart in the … meant to call in, but…nuisance…terrible times… " – until they got off the bus at the lane. "Come in and make you a nice cup of tea, shall I?"

"I think mummy would like to lie down, now," said Kate in her most grown-up voice.

Mrs. Evans chuckled. "Right you are. I'll call in tomorrow to see how you are, then," and she went off up the lane while Liz struggled with the bag and the door key.

Kate went straight in and turned on all the lights, "To make it look cosy," she explained to her mother.

They unpacked the bag together, putting Mrs. Phillips' shopping aside for the next morning. "She won't mind," said Kate.

"Let's sit down," said Liz at last. They sat on the sofa with their new books, although Liz for once wasn't in the mood for reading. She felt exhausted and unsure of herself. She mustn't ever do such a thing again. Poor Kate! What must she have thought?

Kate leaned over and gave her a hug. "It was the butcher's fault," she said.

"What do you mean?"

"What he said," Kate explained. "He asked you about Nan and Gramps, and Ben, and you got reminded and sad."

"No," replied Liz. "It was the lamb chops. Ben's favourite. And I was so pleased about the money, and it was such fun shopping. And I pictured cooking for all of us…"

"I don't mind if you cry for Ben," said Kate.

"Do you cry for him?" Liz asked curiously.

Kate nodded. "I cry in my tent," she said. "Not so much now – he must be getting nearer."

"Yes, he must be," said Liz. "Come on – let's go and cook for us, and hope Ben is having a good feast, too, where ever he is."

Kate followed Liz to the kitchen. "I think he's in Wales, now," Kate said into the fridge, looking for the chops. "He's not here yet because he didn't find my note, but I can use it again for if we go out again and he comes."

"Of course you can, my love," said Liz, smiling and hoping.

10

Ben stood up and gazed round. Towards the end of the field there was a wood – as good a place as any to aim for.

It was an ancient wood, with twisted lichen-covered trees. The ground was thick and bright with moss, and each tree seemed to preside over its own small area of flowers and rocks, the canopy green and welcoming, and shot through with late-afternoon sun. Ben felt himself unknot. There was the welcome sound of water – a small stream splashed between roots and stones and dripped from rocks. He stripped off the filthy anorak and sweatshirt and dragged them to and fro in the clear water until they looked clean. Then he undressed and washed himself. The water was soft and silky and cold, and it felt good to get rid of the sweat and grime of the last few days. He shivered, so he rubbed himself nearly dry with his pants and socks, then rooted about in the rucksack until he found clean ones. He spread the wet anorak over a stone and put the sweatshirt and his dirty clothes carefully into a plastic bag. Mum would be proud of me, he thought, grinning to himself.

He pictured his mum and Kate in the Welsh house. He saw his mother sitting by the fire, reading and listening to the radio, and Kate, building little houses and camps – under the stairs, in the shed, by the apple tree – then his mother in the kitchen, chopping and cooking, and feeding Kate bits of raw carrot or pastry… He was so hungry!

Dressed and dry, Ben fished about in the rucksack to see what he had left. The remains of the Spam had been squashed and looked dodgy, so he dug a little hole by a tree root and buried it. There was a bag of noodles, that needed cooking, a tin of butter beans with a ring pull, and a very small tin of anchovies that he had forgotten about. He made himself comfortable against a twisted tree trunk, and opened the butter beans. He'd always refused to eat them – "Too claggy – boring!" he'd protested. Now, on an empty stomach, they had a pleasant starchy quality that filled and soothed him like mashed potatoes. He decided to keep the anchovies for later; he didn't feel quite well enough for anything so strong-tasting. He finished the beans and took the tin to the stream to rinse it out, then drank long gulps of stream water from the tin. Useful. He wondered briefly whether the water was safe, and deciding he didn't care, drank some more.

What to do next? It wasn't wise to keep walking as the sun went down, though he'd eventually have to get back to a road. He opened the AA book, and tried to find out where he was. The man been on the way to Carmarthen, then turned off to the left. But where, exactly? He only knew the main roads. He squinted at the map in the fading light, trying to remember the shape of the road, landmarks like farms or bridges. He had managed so well so far, until that bastard… He needed the proper Ordnance Survey maps that he had stupidly left in London. He leapt up and stomped about, kicking rocks and trees. What a crazy place to end up in. The end of his great plans. He didn't want to be lost in a wood, however small, however beautiful. He hurled himself to on the ground, squirmed round until he found a comfortable pillow of moss, and cried himself to sleep.

When he awoke he raised a hand to block out the sunlight shining in his eyes. It took some moments to realise the sun didn't bob about like that. Someone was shining a torch in his face.

Ben leapt to his feet and crouched against the tree trunk, snatching at the strap of his rucksack. "No! No!" he croaked. "I won't go! I'll get there by myself – get away from me!"

There was a dry chuckle, and the torch was lowered. "I don't want to take you anywhere, don't worry. Just want to know what you're doing in my wood?"

By the light of the torch, Ben could just discern rough jeans and layers of grubby t-shirts, dreadlocks and straggly beard. Ben gave a sob, half laughed. Surely not twice in two days? He shivered and his stomach lurched.

"Well?" prompted the man, watching him closely. "See, for all I know, you might be a Runner, and I don't want the Cleaners here, trampling their filthy great boots over my plants and animals." The man paused for a moment, staring intently. "Come with me!" he said suddenly, as though he had made up his mind. Before Ben could think about running, he was grabbed by one strong hand, while the other hand lifted Ben's possessions.

"No! Please don't. I'll go – I won't tell anyone…" Ben's legs went weak.

"Tell anyone what? I'm not the one in the wrong – this is my wood, and I don't like strangers in it, see? Now, you come in here with me, and we'll have a conversation like sensible people, right?" As he spoke, he pushed Ben under a low wooden archway, between trees. They entered a wide room with a stamped earth floor, and walls of wood and wattle-and-daub. The man pushed Ben down on a length of tree trunk, lit a small oil lamp, then sat cross-legged opposite.

"Story time," he announced. "You start."

Ben hesitated, then, Oh, what the hell! he thought, and slowly, with many repetitions and pauses, he began his story: the escape from school, the train journey, the "lift" in the brewers' lorry… As he got to the car ride, his voice shook until he was almost whispering. He stopped.

"There are always the bad ones," said the man. "At least you had the wit to get away."

Ben shrugged. "And luck," he said.

The man nodded. "But you have to take advantage of luck when it arrives. Look at you – you got away from the Cleaners, and the station guy, and the groper… I hadn't realised life was getting so dangerous everywhere," he ended, thoughtfully. "And things change so quickly in London…"

"You're from London, aren't you?" Ben asked, catching something in the man's accent. "Why are you here?"

"Easy – I came years ago, before the sickness started: don't like towns, don't like people, do like trees and quiet." He gave Ben a long look. "I could give you a hand if you think you can trust me. You're probably not a Carrier – what do you think?"

Ben looked at him. "I'm Ben," he said eventually. "Who are you?"

"In the village they call me Woodman, but Rufus is my name. Now we must sleep, Ben. We'll make some plans in the morning." Rufus had a sleeping place opposite the entrance, on a pile of bracken.

Ben, rolled up in an old blanket that Rufus had produced from a bag hung on the wall, breathed in the smells of wood smoke and earth, until he forgot his journey, and finally fell asleep.

He slept and slept. Once, he was dimly aware of birdsong, and a sweet smell of leaves and dampness carried on the cool air. He wriggled tighter into the blanket and slept again. Later he heard footsteps padding about on the earth, and fear shot through him. He sat up.

"Thought I'd let you sleep your sleep out," said a voice. "Now, eat this," and Rufus handed him a wooden bowl of stew and a wooden spoon. "Cawl, that is," he said. "Good medicine."

Ben wanted to say that he didn't need medicine, when he saw Rufus serving himself from the iron pot which hung from a tripod, outside the room's entrance. He waited until he saw Rufus eating, then took a mouthful himself. It was delicious. It was a long time since he had eaten hot food. When his bowl was empty, he waited to be offered more, but Rufus put a lid on the pot and handed his bowl and spoon to Ben. "You can do the dishes," he said, pointing in the direction of the stream.

Ben rubbed the bowls and spoons with grass, then rinsed them in the running water and shook them dry. He took them back to Rufus, who grinned at him. "You in the Scouts?" he asked.

Ben shook his head. "*Boy's Book of Woodcraft.*"

"Nothing but the best!" said Rufus. "I should know – I wrote some of it," he said. "Writer, woodman, woodcarver… Secret is to do what you can and what you like. What do you like?" he asked Ben suddenly.

Ben said nothing.

"You don't know yet, do you?" said Rufus. "Wait till you get safe home and you'll start getting some ideas. But home first, right?"

Ben nodded. "Could you – I mean, do you think – you see, I don't know where…"

"Spit it out! Ask a plain question, and I'll give you a straight answer!"

"Can you give me a lift? I mean, I don't know how far it is, and when we get there, mum would pay you for the petrol, I know, and …"

Rufus shook his head. "No," he said.

Ben's eyebrows shot up. Rufus roared with laughter.

"Why not?" asked Ben.

"Because I can't be arsed, I could get picked up for kidnapping a minor, or rescuing a Runner, and I've only got a bicycle."

"Oh," said Ben. His vision of being home by the end of the day shimmered and burst.

Rufus laughed again. "Don't do cars or phones or televisions…"

"There aren't any, any more," Ben interrupted. "Well, cars, but there's not much petrol…"

"So much the better! Something good will come of all this mess, you'll see." Then, seeing Ben's sad face he added, "but it's all right – you'll get home. I've got maps – look." And from the wall, he unhooked a bag that Ben had taken for a waterproof jacket.

"Ordnance Survey!" cried Ben in delight.

Rufus unfolded the map, smoothing its creases and split edges with gentle hands, and began pointing out the direction Ben needed to follow. Ben found a small notebook in a pocket in his rucksack, and made a rudimentary sketch map of the route. He was glad to see that he was nearer to Carmarthen than he had thought. "Can I borrow the map?" Ben asked. "I'll send you another one…"

"But you might not find another one – who's bothering to print maps at the moment? – apart from the government, and they're not selling. And is the Post Office still functioning? I don't know! You can't count on anything except yourself, now – you've got to look after what you've got!"

Ben blushed. He thought he had done really well so far with the little he had; he wanted Rufus to think well of him, too. He looked at his sketch, and after a nod from Rufus, redrew it more carefully, marking lanes and footpaths clearly, and printing place names legibly.

"Otherwise you'll find yourself walking down the middle of a motorway. And remember now, keep to yourself if you can – quiet ways are best. There are strange people about in these strange times…"

Ben walked down the green lane away from Rufus's wood, the day and the countryside spread out before him, feeling almost happy.

He came to the first junction. He followed his map across a B road, and then down a valley along a stream. The way dwindled to a lane with grass growing down its centre.

He felt glad to be travelling at his own pace, confident of his direction: maps made you feel safe. Home, he thought as he walked. He pictured the lovely shabby Welsh house; Mum and Kate by sitting-room fire, waiting for him, and Kate saying firmly "He'll be here soon…" He didn't know what day it was, nor how long it took to walk a mile, but he was on his way.

He was hungry again. He would just get to – where was it? – and then he would eat. He peered at his map, which looked sketchier than he remembered, and was full of places with lots of l's and w's. Mum would tell him how to pronounce them when he got home. He plodded on. At some point, Rufus had told him, he would have to cross the motorway, which might be dangerous. Not so much because of the traffic, Rufus said, but because he would be so visible in the open, without the sheltering trees and hedges. And you never knew when the Cleaners might be watching.

He thought he would try to get the dangerous motorway section of the journey over first. He quickened his pace.

The road began to broaden; the potholes were fewer. He was no longer walking through green tunnels where branches met overhead. Then the road bent to the left, widened, and there in front of him was the motorway. Ben stood for a moment gazing.

There were a few lorries, but nothing that looked official, nothing with dark windows and hidden number plates. He decided to take a chance. If he charged across the road, he would look as though he were trying to escape, guilty of something. If he ambled across he might look as though he had every right to be there. "But how stupid is that? Who the hell crosses motorways on foot? Oh, well – here goes!"

After a supermarket lorry had passed, he stepped out, and walked casually to the central reservation and climbed over the barrier. No one hooted at him. He strolled across the London-bound side of the road. Nothing.

Perhaps he had just been lucky. Rufus had warned him of danger and risk, but here he was, safely on the other side. He climbed the bank at the edge of the road, crossed a field, found a hedgerow, and sat to eat the food Rufus had given him: a big hunk of home-made bread and a piece of local cheese, in return for which Ben had given the tin of anchovies and the opened bag of noodles.

Ben ate, then had to force himself to continue. He was exhausted, and his father's boot were beginning to rub. He kept going until the long afternoon shadows had disappeared and darkness crept into the lane. He'd get lost if he walked at night. He pushed his way through a gap in the hedge, saw that the field he was in was mercifully free from animals – sheep he didn't mind, but cattle and horses… and camped under a wide and twisted hawthorn tree. He put his extra jumper on, and lay down on his anorak, with the rucksack as a pillow. He slept well.

The next days followed a similar pattern. He walked; ate sparingly from his meagre supply of food; avoided people and animals, and slept. Soon he would have to do something about food. His childhood family walks had taught him about what you should or shouldn't eat, but it was still too early in the year for anything sustaining to be ripe. The few cottages he passed were locked and boarded – holiday lets or second homes. No one went on holiday in these times.

Then he saw it. A large, once-shiny sign tilting by the side of the road: "The Welsh Chocolate Factory", it read, and "Croeso I'r Fferm Siocled Cymraeg". Then a list of prices, and in smaller, curlier writing, "Get the Chocolate Experience – Make your own Hot Chocolate just like the Incas – Personalise your own Chocolate Bar".

Ben could see no one about. The thought of chocolate made his mouth water.

The heavy wooden gate was secured by a rusty chain and padlock. Not surprising – how could a business function in these times, without tourists?

A beaten earth path snaked between gatepost and hedge. Well, someone comes in and out pretty often, Ben thought, and quickly, before he could change his mind, pushed his way through the gap. There was a narrow road, and beyond a line of conifers, a faded-yellow farmhouse squatted in a shallow valley. Some of its windows were broken, and at others, ragged curtains fluttered. The front door was ajar. Ben shivered. It was not a welcoming place. There were outbuildings, that looked like barns, and cowsheds, and workshops; here and there, walls were beginning to crumble, and corrugated iron roofs to rust and slip. Convulvulus and ivy tumbled wildly across buildings and relics from the site's past – picnic tables and benches, fences along paths meant for ramblers, fading signs to "Cocoa Café", "Siop" and "Toiledau". The place looked deserted… but Ben had an uneasy feeling that he was being watched.

He was being ridiculous. He ought to explore the outbuildings and the farmhouse, see if he could find any food, or at least a comfortable place to sleep before moving on. Instead, he made his way slowly across the yard to one of the benches. He eased off his rucksack, and keeping tight hold of the straps, sat down facing the house. He felt as though all the windows were staring him. He sat very still, letting his gaze drift round the scene in front of him: the bright warmth of sun, a tapping of branch on window, a faint breeze, an inside door gently banging…

Footsteps!

Ben leapt to his feet, clutching his bag.

A tall figure crossed the courtyard towards him. It's only a boy, Ben thought, but he stayed put. The boy walked round Ben slowly, several times, peering at him at arm's length, with no expression. Ben tried to meet the boy's eyes, but couldn't keep up with the circling. "Hallo," murmured Ben eventually. The boy stopped his circling and thrust his face towards Ben, who flinched. His breath stank.

"Scared?" asked the boy.

"No," said Ben, lying. He might be a boy, but he was taller and heavier than Ben.

"You a Runner?" the boy asked.

"No!" said Ben, He didn't want the Cleaners after him now he'd come so far.

"Why not?" the boy asked, moving back to stare at Ben again. "Only fools don't Run! You want the Cleaners to get you? You friends with them? You a Carrier, then? You got this sickness? Where have you come from? What's your name? Got any food?" And at each question, he prodded Ben hard in the chest with a bony finger. Then he put two fingers in his mouth and gave a piercing whistle.

At the signal there was a whisper of movement. Where there had been no one, now at each door and window a figure stood. The boy gave Ben a final shove which pushed him to the ground. The figures started to move towards him, slowly and silently, their faces blank, until Ben was encircled. He gazed round him. There were girls as well as boys, mostly older than Ben, and dressed in an odd mixture of grubby white clothing – dirty white wellingtons and plimsolls, overalls, aprons worn in pairs to cover back and front, garments that looked like lab coats. Chocolate factory clothes, Ben realised. They were all very thin; some had long tangled hair, and others had theirs short. Some were tanned and weathered, while others were pale, leaning for support on their companions.

They stared at Ben without speaking.

One of the girls stepped forwards. She looked a bit older than the others, and wore a stiff white cap. She had an almost-clean overall and white rubber clogs.

"Tell!" she commanded.

Ben looked round – yes, she was talking to him.

"I don't know… I mean, what do you want…?" He felt frightened, outnumbered.

"Tell!" she said again, and the people round her began to whisper "Tell! Tell! Tell!" and then fell silent again.

Ben retold his story, school, family, Cleaners, train, kidnap – even Rufus, whom he wanted to keep to himself. And home, where his mother and sister awaited him.

After he finished, there was a buzz of whispering. The boy he had met first was talking seriously to the girl in the hat, throwing unfriendly glances in Ben's direction. He thought he heard the words "Runner", and "Cleaners" several times. He waited.

"Go!" said the girl at last, and Ben stood up, legs wobbling, to leave.

"Not you!" said the girl, in the lilting accent of the area. The young people moved purposefully to the surrounding buildings.

The girl came over to Ben and bent towards him.

"Not true," she said, without aggression.

"But it is true," Ben protested. "All of it! I couldn't make it up! And anyway – why should I?"

The boy wandered over to join in. "She can't understand why you're not a Runner – why you haven't joined a group."

"But I'm going home," Ben protested. "I don't need a group – I'm going home!"

"No home," said the girl, shaking her head.

"She's gone a bit funny since she got the sickness. She thinks everyone gets ill, and then they Run, or they die. Her folks all died – she doesn't understand 'home' any more. But she's really useful here – she wanted to be a nurse – she can organise."

"What about you?" Ben asked. He wasn't sure he wanted to know.

"Oh, I'm sort of second-in-command – I do the heavy stuff. Gardening. Digging. I was going to be a footballer before all this," and he did a little dancing footwork pattern on the rough ground.

"I don't understand," said Ben after a brief silence "Has she had the sickness?"

"Yes," said the boy. "So?"

"But I thought everyone died… I didn't know you could get better…"

"Well, there's better and better, isn't there? Some of them don't die," and he jerked his thumb towards the girl, "but you can't say it does them any good. I think I'd rather die than be like some of them here."

"Why?" asked Ben.

"You've seen them! Some of us can work in the garden and grow stuff to eat – but the rest of them…!"

"What?"

"The rest of them will probably peg it any minute now – they're mostly too daft to look after themselves, apart from her." He laughed. "Some's immune and some's not – luck of the draw, turn of the wheel and all that. Flip a coin and you live – throw a dice and you die," and he did a neat little circle of steps until the girl shoved him and he stopped.

"I think I'd better be moving on," Ben said. He had no idea how to treat this new information, but he felt impelled to get away. "I must go," he repeated. "I need to get home – they're waiting for me."

"Forgotten all about you by now," said the boy.

"Yeah," the girl joined in, "forgotten."

"No!" Ben couldn't remember exactly how long he'd been travelling, but that wasn't possible. These two seemed so certain... Ben stood up, and they both jumped back. "I'm going," he said with more firmness than he felt. He made to leave.

"No need," the boy wheedled. "You're with us now – we can help each other. We're all Runners together, and now we've found a place to stop for a while. We've got a lovely garden here... Grow all our own stuff... You can be our mate – you'll like that! Look, I'm Alfred, and that's Megan – Welsh, see? She helps us with the language. And you ... ?"

"Ben," he said reluctantly.

"And you, Ben, you can help us..." Alfred stopped ad-libbing for an instant; then he was squeezing Ben in a tight shoulder embrace. He was very strong. "What are you good at, Ben?" he asked, increasing the pressure.

Ben's mind went blank. He didn't want to help the Runners.

Alfred gave Ben a shake. "Eh?" he said. "Eh?" He poked him sharply in the arm as he spoke.

"Cooking!" Ben blurted. They probably all cooked for themselves, anyway. "And walking," he added, thinking he could walk to get supplies, perhaps… and walk away.

"Oh, there'll be no more walking," said Alfred, hugging him closer. "You can have a nice rest, now, can't you? And when you've rested, you can help us in the garden, that right, Megan?"

"Yes," said Megan, rearranging her hat. "Gardening'll suit you. And us," she added.

"We all help each other," said Alfred. Still gripping Ben by the shoulders, he marched him across the yard to a stone byre, with a heavy wooden door. "You can live in here for a bit," he said. "It's nice and comfortable."

"We'll bring food," said Megan, as if this would be a great treat.

Ben suddenly squirmed violently beneath Alfred's grip. "I want to go home!" he yelled. "I don't want to stay here!"

Alfred promptly got him in a headlock, kicked open the door, and threw him inside. "We'd like you to stay," he said. "You'll like it, I promise you."

Before Ben's eyesight could adjust to the dimness of the barn, he heard a key turning in the lock.

"Food soon," said Megan as if there were nothing unusual about locking up a passing traveller.

"Have a little nap," said Alfred. "Make you feel better."

Their feet crunched away across the farmyard.

11

Ben was constantly in their minds. Liz was hopeful, but Kate seemed absolutely certain that Ben was on his way. She had made a collection of treasures from the garden – a skeleton leaf, a seagull feather, a piece of shiny black basalt – which she arranged with care on Ben's chest of drawers. "Ben's museum," she called it.

They both tried to keep busy. In the evenings, Liz listened to music or the radio, patched and let down hems on Ben's old jeans, even darned holes in his jumpers and socks. If she found herself worrying – why hadn't Ben arrived yet? – What about Kate's school? – she read books, any she could find, to keep her mind occupied. Her father had had an eclectic collection of tapes, from Mozart to Welsh male voice choirs, and an old machine to play them on. From the depths of her father's battered old leather armchair, Liz and Kate would warble along to "Sospan fach" and "Bread of Heaven". Kate picked up the Welsh words quickly, Liz noted, pleased.

They had visitors, too. Mrs. Phillips sometimes called, refusing all offers of tea or coffee. "No – you keep your rations – just come to see how you're getting on."

She'd sit down next to Kate, and flourish her notebook and pencil. "Here you are," she'd say to Kate. "You can help me write my shopping list, if you'd like to." Kate wrestled with spellings with words like "semolina", "sardines" and "Bovril". When Kate's concentration strayed, she'd beg her to write a list of reminders. "I'm so forgetful! 'Dust picture frames. Shake rugs. Weed cabbages.' That'll keep me in order!"

"Really?" Kate asked.

"Of course!" said Mrs. Phillips. "Always need a list to remember the boring stuff. Isn't that so?" She turned to Liz, who nodded. "No news yet?" she asked quietly, and Liz shook her head.

Mrs. Phillips helped Kate correct her writing, and folded the pages tidily together. "I pin these to the kitchen wall," she said. "Helps me enormously."

"Wouldn't help me," said Kate when she'd gone.

"That's because you're young," said Liz.

"You don't have lists everywhere, and you're old," said Kate.

"I know… Suppose you made a book for Ben – a sort of handbook, you know? Like, where to find his clothes, or what the things in the museum are, and the shortest way to get into town…?"

"And I could make pictures to explain things," she said.

"Exactly!" said Liz. "You could do a little bit every day, so it'll be ready…" Anything to fill in time.

Another visitor was Mari Evans, who, true to her word, had dropped by after Liz's High Street breakdown, and now popped in regularly.

"Just thought I'd look in. Anything you want up at Cyril's, now? Not that he's got a lot, mind you – can't think what Bethan saw in him, and she could have had Jones the Post, or that Dafydd from the mill. Fancy an outing to town, then? Only I could do with a trip to the market – see what they've got…"

"Have some tea before you go," Liz said. "We're all right at the moment – did a big shop not long ago."

Kate appeared. Tea for visitors meant biscuits, too. "I'd like to go into town," she said. "I want to buy some writing paper and envelopes so I can write to people, like Nan and Gramps…"

"But, my love, you know… I'm not sure the post works any more, anyway…"

"Only pretend!" Kate spluttered biscuit crumbs.

"Oh, well, maybe next time we go…" Liz began.

"She could come with me now, if you like. We'll be fine, won't we?" Mari said. "Give you a bit of peace and quiet, Mrs. P. Not much of that about with a little one, and she'll be a bit of company for me, won't you?"

Kate nodded, bright-eyed.

Liz was caught. Would Mari be careful enough? She might stuff her with sweets and fizzy drinks like she did her grandchildren.

"Oh, no," she began. "We can go another day – I don't want to bother you…"

"But, Mummy…"

"She'll be no bother, now, will you, cariad? And we'll be back on the five o'clock bus."

"Well, I suppose…"

"Thanks, Mum! – can I have some money? Please," she added. "And I will be good."

"I know you will," said Liz.

"Of course she will," said Mari. "Come on, now ! We'll have a bit of fun, won't we?"

They left in a flurry of money and purses, and jackets in case of rain.

It was good to have the house to herself for a while. It was nearly three o'clock now. She'd do the washing, brush the stairs – the hoover had given up ages ago – and clean the bath. Mrs. Phillips had explained the merits of bicarb. as a cleaner, a trick from wartime days. It was maybe worth a try, and cheaper… Or she could read, one of the books she'd bought on what she thought of as "breakdown day".

Someone had told her what a page-turner this book was, how you couldn't put it down. Liz found she could put it down, and did so several times. She made tea, and then a sandwich she didn't really want. She spent a long time washing her hands and putting cream on her face. She looked thinner and hollowed-out. She wanted to phone someone – one of her old friends from London, her mother, Ben. Ben was dreadful on the phone, monosyllabic and curt.

She needed to get busy.

So when Mari banged on the door just after half past five, Liz was upstairs washing sheets in the bath. When she finally heard, she dashed down with a welcoming smile on her face. "Tea!" she said, flinging the door open. "Come in and…" She looked round for Kate. Was she hiding? She liked to do that, give you a scare, then jump out at you.

Mari's face was scrunched up and angry, and swollen as if she had been crying.

"I told her," she was saying. "I told her to stay right there while I popped in the chemist for a moment. Gwilym was asking about you, and when I got out… she was gone…"

Liz sat down at the bottom of the stairs.

"Gone. Gwilym said get the police. I said they won't move till it's been at least a day – and anyway she's most likely just run on home. She back yet?"

Liz hadn't not moved. She was shivering.

"Sorry, sorry… didn't mean… happen to anyone… all come right…"

"You came home and left my daughter in town," she said

"But I looked – I asked…"

"Not enough," said Liz. "I'll find her."

"But there's no more buses…"

Liz got up and walked towards the door. Mari backed away.

"What can I do?" she moaned. "I didn't mean it."

Liz ignored her. She unhooked the car keys from the shelf by the door, and grabbed her handbag.

The car started first time.

She backed the car through the gates, and drove into the village. It was strange to be driving again. She stopped outside Cyril's.

"Double yellow!" Cyril came out to tell her. "Oh, it's you, then. Same rules in Wales as in England."

"Have you seen Kate?" Liz asked.

"What? She escaped then?"

"Have you seen her?" she asked again.

Cyril shook his head. "Bethan!" he called. "Have we seen Mrs. P.'s little girl anywhere?"

Liz didn't wait to hear. She pulled out and headed towards the town.

There was little traffic. She drove at a crawl in second gear, eyes darting from side to side, now and then stopping to peer into a driveway or front garden. She parked at the supermarket by the river. She ran to the High Street, looking into all the shops as she went. The Bank was closing; Mr. Morgan was on his way out.

"Have you seen my little girl?"

Mr Morgan shook his head, recognised Liz, and said, "Not since..."

Liz hurried on. She searched each shop that might appeal to Kate: the toy shop, the stationer's, the Pound Shop, and then the chemist's. Gwilym rushed forward to greet her, his face creased with concern. "Found her yet? Only a few minutes she was in here – Mari, that is

– beside herself! 'What's Mrs. P. going to think of me?' she was saying. And we all looked… Not a sight of her!"

"Thank you," Liz said. She went on round the town, scouring the alleyways, courtyards and backs of shops. Finally she went to sit on the bench outside the Market Hall. It was a local meeting-place. She and Michael had often met up there when the children were little – would Kate think of it? She waited for what seemed a long time. She asked people: "A little girl, seven, brown hair and jeans and a red raincoat…" Someone said, "Yes, I saw her with Mari Evans this afternoon – oh, no, not by herself…"

She's such a sensible child, Liz thought. She wouldn't do anything stupid.

But someone else might.

She returned to the car park. "Oh, Kate!" She leant against the car and wept, tearing a parking ticket that had been left on the car into tiny pieces that she threw in the river. They floated like dead leaves on the dark water.

Perhaps she was at home already, wondering where her mother was, gone to ask Mrs. Phillips. Liz started the car. Dusk was falling. She ought to get home before dark – she'd put all the lights on, as Kate had done, to make it cheerful. She'd cook pasta with bacon, Kate's favourite…

Again, she drove slowly, searching. As she approached the second bend in the road before the village, she glimpsed something by the edge of the road

– a small heap of clothes… ? She leapt out of the car and rushed towards the bundle, screaming. "Kate! Kate!"

The bundle sat up. "I was just having a rest," it said. "I'm hungry," she said amid Liz's embraces, tears and questions. "They didn't give me anything to eat."

"Who?" Liz asked fearfully.

"Oh, those kids!" said Kate. "They grabbed me and shut me up and…"

Liz picked her up and buckled her tenderly into the car. "Later," she said. "Home first."

Liz put her sleeping child on the sofa and stroked her hair. Her face was flushed and dirty, and there seemed to be a bruise developing on her forehead. Her hands and arms were dirty and scratched, but no serious damage was visible. She pulled off Kate's trainers and jeans. Kate sighed but slept on. It looked as if she'd been sitting and kneeling in something black, coal dust, perhaps. But nothing was disarranged – buttons and zips still worked in all the right places. Liz kissed Kate's cheek, and left her to sleep. She went to cook the pasta.

Later as they were eating, the story unfolded. With a few prompts from Liz – "Who?" and "Then what?" – Kate staggered through her tale, sometime crying, sometimes furious. It was the village children – "Kids!" Kate called them vehemently – who had found Kate waiting by the chemist's and started to tease. "They said I must be waiting for my medicine, because I had the plague and I'd give it to them if they didn't do something about it…" Kate shivered. "But it was only chicken pox, wasn't it, Mummy? And then they shut me in somewhere…" Kate started to sob again. "There was no light, and I banged and shouted and no one came!" she said with fury. "And me and Mari were going to have tea somewhere, with cake…!"

It seemed that the children, or some of them, must have crept back to undo the coal shed door, and then run away. Kate had heard them sniggering. "And no one came to see if I was all right!"

She had found herself at the back of a pub; made her way back to the High Street; looked briefly into the chemist's, and since Mari wasn't there, decided to walk home. "But I didn't mean to lose Mari, really, mummy…"

"Bath and bed!" Liz said a while later.

She remembered the bath was still full of washing, and she hadn't told Mari that Kate was safe. She put Kate, unwashed, into a clean nightdress, and rocked her asleep.

Downstairs, Liz piled the washing-up into the sink. Children were often nasty to each other, but she sensed something more behind the children's actions. Mimicking their parents, probably – "Don't go near her – she's sick" and "They ought to clear off back to London." She hated being seen as an incomer, bringing the sickness, and using up precious resources, her parents' lives in the village quite forgotten. She scrubbed the frying-pan hard. "We do belong here – Mum and Dad lived here – now it's our home."

The nightmares began later: Kate woke shouting, "Let me out! Open the door!" fighting her way out of her bedclothes. But once awake, she calmed down quickly, and by next day had forgotten.

After a few days, Mari visited, full of apologies, bearing a large stuffed doll in a flowery dress – "Belonged to my Lowri, – thought it might keep you company."

Kate was not fond of dolls, but thanked Mari. "You were a long time in that shop," she said, placing the doll beside her on the sofa.

"It's all over and done with, Kate – it was an accident," Liz interrupted.

"Are you having tea?" Kate asked. "Because then we can have biscuits." Liz took the hint and went to the kitchen.

By the time she returned, with biscuits, Mari and Kate were busily talking, and at first Liz struggled to understand. Mari was talking in Welsh about the "doli", and Kate copied her.

"Show your mam what you can do," prompted Mari, and Kate named the doll's body parts, and then counted in Welsh up to ten. "See? We'll make a proper little Welsh girl out of her!"

"That's fantastic, Kate!" Liz said. "Can you teach me?"

They spent the rest of the morning naming things in Welsh.

"Mari," said Liz, as she got up to leave, "do you think you could come again, and teach us some more? Kate needs to learn – I mean, this is our home now, so…"

Mari looked doubtful. "I'm not a proper teacher," she said. "I can't do the book Welsh – just the old chat."

"That's exactly what we need! I mean, I spoke it when I lived here as a child, but I've forgotten so much," said Liz. "I'd really like to get back into it – ask for things in shops, and…"

"Might get more than you bargained for, then – they think you don't understand, they say all sorts of stuff!" Mari laughed.

"We don't want to take exams, Mari, I just want to be able to have a conversation – show that I belong – Kate, too, don't you?" she appealed to her daughter.

"Croeso y Cymru," said Kate.

"And the same to you!" said Mari, giving her a hug. "Of course I'll help you if I can!… All better now?"

"All better," said Liz, nodding.

Though it wasn't all better. She was still sick with worry about Ben, out there somewhere, on his own.

After Mari had gone, Liz cried quietly into her lunchtime soup. Kate's arms came round her waist.

"You're crying for Ben, aren't you?"

"I'm sorry," Liz admitted.

"It's fair," said Kate. "You cried for me, too, didn't you? Perhaps Ben's got himself caught by some horrible kids, as well, but he won't take long to get away. And then he'll soon be here!"

"Of course he will," Liz said.

12

Ben yelled and kicked at the door until his feet hurt and his hands were scratched. No one came. It was a solid door of ancient black wood, unyielding as iron. A narrow metal grid just under the roof cast the only available light, revealing wooden partitions along one side of the byre where cows must have stood to be milked. Bales of old hay were piled in a corner on the stone-flagged floor.

Ben crept round and round his prison, hands feeling along the solid walls, feet kicking aside the hay in hopes of disclosing some means of escape. Nothing. A corner of the floor sloped down to a drain, far too small to escape through, but useful as a lavatory, if he were kept here long. As he tried to think up plans, he saw Mum and Kate waiting for him. How could he have been so stupid – that word "chocolate" luring him, when he knew there couldn't be any? He should have left while he thought the farm was empty, instead of hanging about.

He threw himself on to the pile of hay. He'd been lucky so far, but he had no idea what to do next.

He slept.

Daylight oozed through the gaps under the eaves. Next to him, on a bale of hay, was a bowl and a spoon. The bowl contained some kind of thick soup – a bit like his Nan's lentil soup – studded with vegetables. Ben was ravenous. The soup was cold, but tasted delicious. After he'd finished it he wondered who'd left it there. It had been far better than the manky bit of old bread that was all he had left. He was going to be a well-fed prisoner. Then he remembered the strength of Alfred's grip round his shoulders. He'd have to scheme, not fight, his way out.

A key scraped, and the heavy door swung open, letting in wide bar of sunlight.

"Good weather for gardening," said Alfred cheerfully. "Are you up yet?"

Since Ben hadn't undressed the night before, he had to admit that he was. "What now?" Ben said. "I want to go home – they're waiting for me."

"So you keep saying. Ever thought that they might not have made it? Picked up by the Cleaners on the way down? Caught the bug and pegged it? Set on by locals? Anything's possible!" he jeered, grabbing Ben by the shoulder and marching him into the yard.

Ben rubbed his eyes against the sun and the tears that threatened to fall. "I must go home,"

"We'll see," said Alfred, sounding for moment like Ben's father. "Here's Megan – she'll show you what to do."

Megan drifted across the yard, scuffing her clogs.

She ringed one hand round Ben's wrist, led him round to the back of the house, where there was an enormous walled garden. Alfred was right – it was a lovely garden, full of vegetables in leaf, in flower, and some in fruit. Ben recognised pea and courgettes plants, and lettuces and tomatoes. It was like his Grampa's allotment only much bigger.

"Food," announced Megan. "Some to eat – some to sell."

"What do you want me to do?" asked Ben.

There were figures in the garden working industriously, weeding, tying up, picking and planting. And digging. There were other figures round the edge of the plot, sitting on the grass, and on benches and up-turned flower pots. Those that worked were tanned and healthy-looking, like Alfred and Megan. Those who watched were pale and thin, and moved with difficulty, like frail invalids forced out for fresh air.

"Who are they?" Ben said. "Why are they there?"

"They work," Megan said. "Others sit in the sun. While they can."

"Then what?"

Megan shrugged. "They're the dying ones," she said. "No use until – "

Alfred appeared behind them and prodded Ben.

"Not working yet?" He handed Ben a small fork. "Know what a pea looks like?"

Ben nodded.

"Weed those rows of peas," he said. "Don't want any

aliens climbing our nice pea sticks, do we? And mind where you tread with those great boots!"

Ben began to dig out anything that was not pea-like. It took a long time.

After what seemed hours of back-breaking work, he straightened up to look round. The other gardeners were still labouring. Some of the sick ones had disappeared; some of the more fragile were helping each other into the shade.

"Gets too much for them, even watching work," said Alfred, just behind him. Ben dropped the fork in surprise, and Alfred's boot nudged him hard as he bent to pick it up.

Ben turned. "Look, I don't have to stay here, you know. I don't mind helping you a bit in return for food, but I've got to get – "

"You've got to get home – yes, I know. But supposing we need you, eh? You're just the sort of bloke who could sell stuff in the market without putting the locals off. And you're strong and healthy, so far – "

"What do you mean, so far? You think I'll die, like…" And he gestured at the sick ones as they shuffled indoors.

"I don't think anything much," said Alfred. "I can't tell what's going to happen to you. You may be immune, like me, or you may be a recoverer like Megan, and some of the workers. But everyone's useful, in their way…"

"What – even the dead ones?" sneered Ben.

"Oh dear me – deary, deary me." Alfred pulled a face. "For such a posh little boy, you really don't catch on very quick, do you? Dead ones are the most use of all. Wrap 'em in a bit of old curtain, bury 'em deep, and there they are – pouring their hearts and souls and bodies into the goodness of the earth. Takes time, mind you – takes time. We've been here a few years now, and we're just beginning to see the benefits. We're in it for the long term, we are. And you could join us, see? You could be a big help – we don't get so many healthy Runners now, so it gets harder to keep up with the dying." He punched Ben on the arm matily.

"You want me to help…?"

"Bury people – that's right. Only when they're properly dead, of course," and Alfred snorted at his little joke. "Well, someone's got to," he added defensively. "Years back we got sick of moving on when someone died. Then we found this place, and it was all sorted. Except we do run out of diggers now and then. What do you say, now you see the logic of it all?"

Ben breathed the sweet clean air. He wouldn't mind the planting and growing…

"And of course," Alfred's voice went on, "no one's got time or money for fertiliser, so we have to…"

I must get home, Ben was thinking. But I mustn't antagonise Alfred and Megan. Ben's hands trembled as he clutched the fork.

"But I've never seen anyone dead," he blurted "I wouldn't know what to do…"

"That's what I'm here for," said Alfred.

He gripped Ben tightly by the upper arm, part guided, part propelled him out of the garden, along a rough path. "Just going to show him," Alfred called as they passed Megan sorting vegetables in front of the house. She waved affably.

"Look, I really want to go home," Ben tried again. " I don't want… I haven't ever… I have to go…"

They arrived at a low corrugated iron building, with no windows and a secure-looking metal door which Alfred pushed open. The smell was appalling. "You get used to it," said Alfred, gripping his arm tighter. Ben vomited.

"You're not the first," said Alfred, and dragged Ben further in. "This is where we keep them,"

There were five or six bodies, all young, scantily covered with old bits of cloth: curtain, sheet, scarf. Ben made himself look. Most of the faces were exposed: some seemed to be asleep, except for their strange pallor, while others grimaced as though struggling. Here and there an arm or leg protruded from the cloth, white and waxy, or dark and mottled. He threw up again.

"They're only dead," said Alfred. "They can't hurt you."

"What about germs?" Ben asked, between retching and spitting.

Alfred shrugged. "I've told you – either you get it or you don't – dead or alive makes no difference. And all we do's help them keep helping us."

"Right," said Ben at last.

"You mean right, you'll join us? Or right, you see what I'm getting at, but…"

"But," said Ben, with more courage than he felt. "Who do they belong to? Where are their families? Don't you have to tell someone when somebody dies?"

"Not any more," said Alfred. "Who's to check? These kids ran away, probably when their families died. If they belong to anyone, it's us – we looked after them, didn't we?"

Ben bowed his head, suddenly overwhelmed with sorrow. "What do you want me to do?" he said.

Alfred put his arm round him, gripping tightly.

"I knew you'd see it our way!" he said, "because you know what? You're clever, you are – I could tell straight away. This is the lad to join the management team, I thought – soon as I saw you! Come on, then – let's get started!"

"Get hold!" commanded Alfred, sliding his hands under the body's shoulders.

Ben saw he was expected to help Alfred lift a body onto a flat trolley parked nearby. He pulled a bit of cloth round the ankles so he didn't touch the dead flesh.

"Get on with it!" barked Alfred, so that Ben jumped, and his hands closed round cold thin bones.

By the time they had loaded three more bodies, Ben was managing better. "They're only dead," he told himself. "They can't help it."

They wheeled the trolley back along the path to a far corner of the garden, where a couple of strong-looking

Runners were shovelling the earth.

"Customers!" called Alfred, and the two diggers climbed out of the pit and started to unload.

Ben's new found bravura drained away. "No breath… no sight… I can't cover them – I can't!" One of the diggers handed him a spade and Ben started helping as though he'd always been a gravedigger. "Don't antagonise…" he told himself.

The bodies were laid with some care at the bottom of the pit.

"They were our friends," said Alfred, and the work went on with a rhythm as the four lifted and covered, until all you could see was earth.

Days and weeks passed. Every night Alfred or Megan locked him up. Every day Ben was let out to lift, carry and bury bodies. Every day he determined to make a plan, and every day he failed. The work was becoming a dreadful kind of normality, and to his horror he found he was getting used to the routine, the smells, the bodies. He was pleased when Alfred praised him for filling a pit quickly, or when Megan smiled and nodded at him. Some of the other workers chatted to him, as well; they passed the time of day, or simply complained about the rain.

"I'd rather be digging for gold in the mountains," one would say.

"I'd rather be digging out rabbits for pie," said another.

"What about you, Ben?" someone asked.

"Oh, he'd rather be digging sandcastles at Tenby!" And they laughed. A sense of camaraderie was growing, along with the vegetables.

13

Ben was now allowed to eat with everyone else, in the large kitchen of the farmhouse. The trouble was, he'd lost his appetite. He saw the poor sick emaciated creatures, trying to force down morsels of food, then the healthy sunburned ones, shovelling food in as if someone were about to steal it. It was good food, too – fresh vegetables, as Megan liked to remind them, all home-grown. Home-grown – over the bodies laid at the bottom of each pit… He'd manage a slurp of soup, a bite of cabbage or spinach, but anything that grew underground – potatoes, carrots – made him sick.

He knew he was getting thinner, and weaker. He was relieved to be locked into the byre each night. He had a lot of time to plan his escape and he wasn't sleeping much, in spite of the physical exercise. His sleep, when it came, was punctuated with dreams of bodies rippling with maggots – "Maggots are normal – maggots helped break down the flesh," Alfred had told him. But they wriggled through his thoughts and dreams, and his brain refused to plan.

One morning as the door was being unlocked, he found he couldn't move. He burrowed further down into his straw bed, too weary to lift his eyelids. As if from a distance, Alfred's voice called through the doorway. "Get up, you lazy bastard! It's work time!" His boots clunked away, and Ben slept again.

Then he felt Alfred's hands pulling him roughly out of the straw and setting him on his feet. Ben tottered, then started to pull his clothes on.

"Christ! I've seen corpses look better! Megan! Get over here! Have a look at this!"

Ben heard the scuffing of Megan's clogs over the stones, and then her head poked round the door. She gave Ben a long look. "So?" she said eventually.

"Well, he's not right, is he?" Alfred said. "Has he...?"

"No," said Megan scornfully. "Don't want to work." She approached Ben and peered into his eyes. "I'm a nurse," she hissed, as Ben backed away from her probing fingers. She gripped him by the arm, then punched him in the belly.

Ben collapsed back on to the straw. "Why?"

"Too thin," said Megan to Alfred. "No good to us thin."

"We'll just have to feed him up, then, won't we?" And Alfred hauled Ben up again, and supported him out of the byre and into the kitchen. "Make him eat," he told Megan. "Something soft and easy."

She approached Ben with a bowl and a spoon. "Lovely soup," she crooned. "Lovely potato soup." She put the spoon in Ben's hand, and he immediately set it down.

"Eat!"

Ben shook his head and tightened his lips.

Megan took up a spoonful of soup, and tried to poke it into Ben's mouth.

Ben swerved, and the soup went down his neck.

Megan slapped him, hard, across his ear. "Eat!" she said again. This time she held Ben's nose, and as his mouth opened, forced the spoon in.

Ben spat the soup out, and heaved.

Megan tried the tactic again, and this time Ben was sick over the bowl. "Ach y fi!" she screamed, and Alfred, who had watched closely, gestured with a sideways nod of his head that Megan was to leave. He fetched a mug of water, and Ben gulped it down gratefully.

"Now, what's all this about?" Alfred sat at the table next to Ben without touching him. "Come on – say your piece."

Ben shook his head. "Can't," he said after a pause.

"Can't what?" prompted Alfred.

Ben's lip was bleeding where Megan had forced the spoon in. "Can't eat," he murmured.

"That'll soon clear up – she gets a bit irritated if someone crosses her – doesn't mean to do any damage," and Alfred nudged Ben encouragingly.

Ben sighed. It was too difficult. "Can't eat," he tried again. He didn't want to either: he'd accidentally found a good way to get out – he would just refuse to eat until he faded away. He would turn into maggots and vegetables, and that would be an end of it…

"You're not going to die on us?" Alfred inquired, as if reading his thoughts. "What about all your little plans, eh? I know you've got plans – see your mum, and your – sister, was it?" Alfred sounded almost kind.

Ben shook his head. His mother and Kate seemed far away. He tried to picture them; the images kept sliding away. It would be so easy just to give up, Ben was thinking. No more travelling. Suddenly a picture of Kate materialised, sharp and clear as glass – Kate in the garden of the Welsh house, looking up and down the road, her horrible bit of blanket clutched in her hand. And behind her was his mother, looking somehow smaller and paler than he remembered.

Alfred was still talking.

Ben shook his head again.

"So you're not going to play the game?" Alfred was asking.

Ben gazed at Alfred's intent face. He couldn't imagine why Alfred should care what he did. "Don't want to stay here," he muttered.

"There's nowhere else," said Alfred savagely. "There'll be no one in your precious little house – no mum, no sister. This is all there is – work and food and safety. No one to bother us."

"But they are there, and I want to go home," he said, with great certainty. "I know they're there, and even if they're not, it's still my home. I can wait for them… just stay there…" Ben's words trailed off, watching Alfred's expression, as disbelief, greed, and longing flickered across his face.

Alfred rose, and walked round and round the table, every so often approaching Ben as if to say something, then shaking his head and continuing his circling. Ben watched, clinging to the image of Kate and his mother.

Alfred scraped a chair across the floor and sat opposite Ben. "I'll tell you what we'll do," he said.

Ben said nothing.

"I'll take you there!" He leant back on the chair and looked at Ben triumphantly.

There had to be a catch.

"No, honest!" said Alfred. "I'll take you home, and if no one's there, we'll come back here and settle down properly. Right? And there might be some stuff in your place that we could do with here, right…?

Really? Ben was thinking. I'm really going to walk out of here with Alfred as my guide? How can it be that easy? But he remembered the expressions on Alfred's face… And finally nodded. If they've arrived, he figured, Alfred wouldn't stand a chance – Mum knows people… And if they hadn't… Ben went cold at the thought – well, he'd just have to make something up.

"When shall we go?" Ben asked.

Alfred whooped and raised his hand to high-five. "And I thought you were at death's door! Wonderful what getting your own way'll do for you! I'll have to square it with Megan first, then we'll be off. Get your stuff together! – Oh, and eat this. Don't want you dying on me now!" He handed Ben a chunk of bread and some cheese, which Ben nibbled at, then thrust into his pocket.

He went to the byre to pick up his rucksack, rolling his anorak tightly to fit inside.

As he waited in the yard, he half-expected Alfred to come back and tell him it was all a joke, that he must get out to the garden and get working. Voices came from the room above the kitchen, Alfred, smooth and reasonable, and Megan, shouting in Welsh.

"Didn't understand a word," said Alfred appearing suddenly at Ben's side. "But she's not best pleased. Says we put a lot of work into you and haven't had our money's worth yet – still, we will, won't we? I said you'd be bound to have lots of good stuff... Come on, then – let's go before she changes her mind!"

And Ben, terrified of losing the chance to get out, shouldered his bag, and followed.

14

"You do know the way?" asked Alfred, when they were well away from the Chocolate Farm.

"Sort of," said Ben, not wanting to get out the notes he'd made from Rufus's map. He didn't want Alfred to see the route. He concentrated on visualising his map and fending off Alfred's increasingly specific questions.

"So, how many rooms has your house got?" and "You got the central heating, of course," and "How many bathrooms? Can't have too many bathrooms," until Ben said, "You want to buy it? Because it's not for sale!"

"Not buy, exactly," was the reply. Alfred was quiet for the next few miles.

They walked on, keeping to narrow grassy roads. Alfred was beginning to get restless. "You sure you know where you're going?" he asked several times.

"West," replied Ben, more firmly than he felt.

"So where's West?" asked Alfred suspiciously.

"This way," said Ben, pointing.

"How do know that?" Alfred was getting annoyed.

Boy's Book of Woodcraft, Ben wanted to say. "I just do."

Alfred shrugged.

They were walking towards the setting sun, so Ben was confident about the direction. They'd been travelling all day, now, and Ben was beginning to stagger with exhaustion.

Eventually Alfred said, "What we going to do, then? I thought we'd be there and back by now – I hadn't planned on camping."

Ben, glad of a break, looked round. There was a hawthorn tree at one side of the road, and a space through to the field. Ben squeezed past the tree. No cattle. Maybe some sheep. "We could sleep here," he called.

Alfred followed, cursing. "Where?"

Ben pointed out the flat dry space under the hawthorn tree, and started gathering armfuls of long grass and cow parsley, and piling it up under the shelter of the tree. He sank gratefully onto one pile, and covered himself with his anorak.

"It's all right for some," Alfred muttered. "You're used to this scouting lark…"

Ben was already asleep.

He woke next morning aching from the hard ground. He managed to eat the remains of the bread and cheese, though the bread was stale and he found swallowing difficult. He didn't feel obliged to save any for Alfred – he'd insisted on this trip, after all, and had come away totally unprepared. Now Alfred woke crossly, stretching and swearing and rubbing his back.

"Let's go," he said, clambering to his feet.

"Okay," said Ben, He rolled up his anorak and stuffed it back in his rucksack. It promised to be another hot day. He followed Alfred back to the road.

Alfred turned to his right and swaggered off.

"That's the way we came," Ben said.

"Just testing, just testing," said Alfred, swinging round on his heel. "You're not bad for a town boy."

On they went. Ben struggled to keep up; he recalled rainy walks with his parents when he was little, his father always in charge of the route, his mother stopping every so often to point out plants – violets, alexanders, ransoms – or curious slate formations, or moss. Kate waved from her carrier on Dad's back; Mum fed them bananas and cartons of juice – they must have gone for miles… or maybe it had just seemed like it.

"Get a move on!" Alfred called. "I don't want to spend another night under a hedge!"

Ben's double-layered socks were wearing thin and holey, and his father's boots were beginning to rub painfully. He was thirsty and wanted to sit down, though they hadn't gone far yet. The idea of a village with a teashop suddenly appealed so much that he wouldn't have minded treating Alfred. Briefly, he found he missed the regular meals at the Chocolate Farm. But not potato soup. Or carrots. Or beetroot… He shuddered.

It was so hot. "Shall we find something to eat or drink?" Ben suggested. "We haven't had anything since yesterday – must be well past lunch-time now."

"Thought you were dieting," Alfred replied. "There'll be stuff at yours, won't there? Can't be long now, eh? Or don't you recognise the old place? Maybe you're just having me on," he said, slowing abruptly so that Ben trod on his heels. "And there isn't any little house, or a little old ma and a little sister…!"

"Where else would I be going? I'm just thirsty," he said.

"And I just want to get there," Alfred said. "Do you know how near we are, yet?"

They were approaching a narrow stone bridge over a swiftly moving stream. Without warning, Ben slid down the bank beside the parapet and scooped the clear water into his mouth. He leant his face to the water, and gulped it in. When he came up for air, Alfred was gazing at him in astonishment.

"How do you know it's not poisonous?" he asked. "Or don't you care? Just another of your little ploys to get out of work?"

"It's clean," said Ben. "Look how clear it is – comes down from the hills."

"Oh, yeah?" said Alfred, but joined him at the edge of the water and put his lips to the surface. He also gulped for a moment, then looked up. "Well, if we both die, it'll be your fault."

Ben shrugged, climbed back up the bank and sat on the parapet waiting. Eggs, he thought – I could eat eggs… or, what was that cheese Mum did with tomatoes? Mozzarella, that was it… or buttered toast – lovely white sliced bread with Marmite…

Something hit his head. Alfred had returned and clouted him hard with the flat of his hand.

"Hey!" Ben shouted, tumbling into the road. He scrambled to his feet. "What was that for?"

The two boys sized each other up for a long moment.

"What?" Alfred looked away. "Just showing you who's boss! Stop you getting ideas. And we need to get a fucking move on! We need to get there and back with the goods, or Megan might take herself off! Though where she'll go, the silly cow…"

Ben didn't care about Megan, but Alfred's frequent mention of "stuff" and "goods" bothered him. Did he really think Ben's home was full of treasure?

"I'm coming," Ben said. He wanted to hit Alfred, though he hadn't the strength or energy for a punch-up. "There's no hurry – the house won't go away."

"But the stuff in it might!" Alfred said. "Haven't you heard of looters? It's what's happening to all the empty places – even down here!"

Ben stood absolutely still. The house couldn't be empty. "What's it got to do with you?" he said finally, while Alfred jittered with impatience.

"I'm not walking all this way for love!" Alfred leaned forward, spat his words in Ben's face. "I got to get something out of it!"

"You said you'd take me home," said Ben stubbornly.

"And I'm taking you home," he shouted. "Unless you've been having me on all this time…?" Alfred threw Ben a menacing glare. "See, I don't know where you live – you could be taking me anywhere…" He gripped Ben's shoulders painfully. "You cheat me, posh boy, and I'll make sure you never see your little house again." He shook Ben hard, knocking him against the parapet.

"I'm coming," said Ben pulling on his rucksack. It felt heavier than before.

It hadn't occurred to him to deceive, he'd been so taken aback by Alfred's agreement to let him go, to accompany him. He hadn't wondered exactly how his mother would deal with Alfred. If she and Kate weren't in the house, how would he manage? Perhaps he could bribe him to go away – but what with? The Welsh house was unadorned, sparsely furnished – no silver or jewellery or art – he couldn't imagine anything that would catch Alfred's magpie eye.

"We going, or what?" Alfred set off again. Ben followed.

So they went on for some time, silently – ignoring each other except when Alfred cursed Ben's flagging pace.

Ben's revulsion for food in recent weeks had weakened him. The idea of Alfred anywhere near his home, whether his mother and Kate were there or not, made him feel ill again. He trudged onwards, ignoring Alfred, who had begun to whinge "Are we nearly there now?"

Like a kid in a car, Ben thought. Alfred was beginning to sound more like the boy Ben had first assumed he was, and less like the boss of a nightmarish vegetable farm. He didn't want Alfred to know where his home was, much less watch him steal from it. He tried to think of a way out, but his mind was blank. He decided to stop trying – they would get to the village and see what happened.

Ben was starting to recognise some of the places they were passing: there was the ford, where his dad had once made him help wash the car; and there was the field of Jacob sheep and the farmhouse where the weavers lived, and here was the narrow valley where an old woman ran a pub from her front room. They were getting nearer – perhaps an hour's car drive away. He didn't say this to Alfred, who was becoming increasingly impatient. He wasn't sure what Alfred was intending to do, but he suspected that nothing he did would benefit Ben. He must stay alert, watch for any opportunity to lose Alfred.

15

Mari called in daily, taking her job as Welsh teacher seriously. She usually came at tea-time, keeping Liz busy each morning making biscuits or cakes. Even Kate was beginning to concede that Mum's baking wasn't too bad.

"Bendigedig!" Kate would say, when Liz presented a new recipe, and Mari would rattle away in Welsh, and Kate would nod wisely.

"Do you really understand all she says?" Liz asked. "Because I can only catch a word or two…"

"Some of it," Kate admitted. "But if I pretend, Mari's happy, and I start understanding a bit more – sometimes I can answer, too!" she added proudly. "Geneth dda, she calls me."

"What does that mean?"

"Don't know, but it's nice," said Kate complacently.

"It means you're a good girl. And you are." Liz laughed. Her own childhood Welsh was coming back to her, and she was glad to see Kate gaining confidence. Though she still hid away in her tents in the garden, she was less tearful, and the nightmares had stopped.

"You seem more cheerful, now, aren't you?" Liz ventured one day.

"Because I know Ben's nearly here."

"Do you now!" Liz longed for her daughter's certainty. "How?"

"I'm going to do my writing now," Kate said, evasively.

This was a new thing. Tired of writing Mrs. Phillips lists and reminders, Kate started to write a story which she posted through Mrs. Phillips' letter-box one day. To her delight, Mrs. Phillips added another chapter, repeating some of some of Kate's words, correctly spelt.

Now that Kate was busier and less demanding, Liz found her mind increasingly preoccupied with Ben – where was he? How was he? Was he getting nearer, as Kate thought? Or was he… She couldn't bear to go on.

She invented her own distractions. Food of all kinds was becoming scarce. At first she'd bought tinned stuff when she could, then that supply dwindled.

"However are we supposed to manage?" she said aloud in despair one day, faced with empty supermarket shelves.

"Grow your own," said a woman next to her. "Have to make do with what's in season, mind, but no worse than when I was a child. You've got a garden. Your Dad used to keep it lovely."

Liz wondered how many more people were going to spring up who knew everything about her.

The old woman was watching her. "Course, you

wouldn't remember me. Auntie Rye, you used to call me, Maria being my name, and you couldn't say that when you were little…"

"Oh, I'm so sorry!" Liz was stricken. She had a distant memory of Auntie Rye baby-sitting her when she was very small – of bright black eyes and raucous laughter. "Of course I remember you!" The eyes hadn't changed a bit, though she was frail now. "And…" Liz hesitated, fumbling for the name, "Edward ?"

There was the laughter. "Oh, yes," she said. "My old Ned's still around, daft old bugger! But if you want a bit of a hand with that garden, now, he's the one. Nothing he can't grow – or so he says! It'll be pineapples in winter, if we listened to you, I tell him! But he'll give you a start, you being Tom's girl."

Liz began to dig.

The garden was an odd triangular shape, higher than the road, and covered with tough field grass. There was the shed, a bay tree, an old, wide-spreading apple tree, and stone steps down to the car space in front of the house. The far side of the triangle was bordered by untidy leylandii, whose sticks and needles fell onto her patch. She remembered her father cursing them. "Shouldn't be allowed," he'd said. "Ground's fit for nothing."

She would have to make it fit.

She went to see Mrs. Phillips.

"Difficult patch to work – but then, you're young and you've got help," she added seeing Liz's glum expression.

"A little at a time, that's the way. Clear a bit and plant it, then move on."

Liz went home full of ideas for easy things to grow – perpetual spinach, tomatoes, potatoes, radishes, lettuces…

She got into a routine of digging and raking the earth each morning, until she had a patch the size of a single bed sheet.

"That's not much!" Kate said in disdain. "Rhy fach!"

"I'll give you too small!" Liz said "You get here and give a hand, and we'll soon see what's small…"

"What can I plant?"

"What about… radishes?"

"Don't like radishes!"

"You will when you've grown them yourself," assured Liz, and Kate, with great ceremony, planted their first crop.

"Mum!" Kate called from the garden one morning. "Someone wants to see you! I think it's a gnome," she whispered loudly.

Liz hurried out. A small, bent, brown-clad man, clasping a sharp-edged spade in one hand and a fork in the other stood by the gate. "Ned!" she said. Auntie Rye had remembered.

Ned nodded. "Come to see your garden. Where do you keep the bugger?"

"I'll show you!" Kate replied.

Liz followed them up the steps.

"This is my bit," Kate was saying. "Radishes, and lettuce."

"Rabbit food!" said Ned scornfully. "Now over here, your Dad – your Grandad – had the potato patch." He gestured to the centre of the garden. "Round the edge were runner beans on sticks – you know." He tented his stiff old fingers to show Kate. "So we need to get rid of this old grass, now…"

"What, all of it?" said Liz in horror, picturing herself spending all day digging.

Ned made a coughing sound that Liz realised was laughter. "Bit at a time," he said. "Bit at a time."

"That's what Mrs. Phillips said," said Kate.

"Oh, well, if Her Ladyship said it, must be right!" He coughed again.

"And what do you charge?" Liz asked.

The old man stuck his spade and fork into the earth violently as if in protest. "Charge?" he said. "I'm doing this for old Tom's girl, and the little one there – seeing as how you knows nothing about anything useful."

"I'm so sorry," Liz said, red-faced. "But I'd like it to be a two-way thing – is there anything I could do for you?"

Ned gave his curious coughing laugh. "That's more like it!" he said. "I wouldn't say no to a little bottle of Felin Foel, now and then. Rye won't have the stuff in the house – brought up strict Chapel…"

"Of course!" said Liz. "That's fine – as long as it won't cause problems…?"

"I'll eat a peppermint: she won't be any the wiser!"

"But we'll know," said Kate," because we'll smell the peppermint, and so will…"

"Bright little thing, eh?" Ned said.

"Geneth dda – that's what Mari says." Kate was showing off.

"Tom would have given the world to see you settled here," said the old man quietly.

"And he did," said Liz.

Ned sniffed loudly, and, grabbing his tools, started hacking away at the field grass.

The change to the garden was gradual, encouraged by the early June sunshine. The neatly cleared beds became greened over with tiny seedlings.

"When can we eat them?" Kate kept asking.

"Don't be daft! You wait," Ned told her.

Thanks to Auntie Rye, they soon had nasturtiums trailing down the sides of the steps. "Leaves are good in salad, and you can pickle the seeds – like capers, you know? Only not too many or you'll get no more flowers."

Mrs. Phillips brought tomato plants. "Pinch out the new growth, and they should fruit by the end of summer."

Ned arrived with yet more seedlings.

"What are they?" Kate asked.

"Peas and beans and spinach," he replied, and showed Kate how to stick canes into the ground in wigwams.

"Little tents!" she said to her mother delightedly.

And soon the seedlings were swarming up their

canes, and the spinach sprouted its first little leaves.

"Can't we pick it yet?" Kate kept asking

"Let it grow a bit more," said Liz, happy her vegetable-hating child was so keen.

Every evening, when it got cooler, they tenderly watered their crops, Kate using her seaside bucket, and Liz a galvanised watering-can she'd found in the shed. They used the washing-up water, washing water, and bath water.

"I wouldn't want to drink my bath water," said Kate, surprised.

"But vegetables don't mind," said Liz. "And we have to use every drop in this heat."

People in the village noticed the transformation. They brought gifts: seedling cabbage, carrots, and even peppers. Once someone left several large straggly plants on the doorstep.

"Whatever are these?" she asked Ned.

"Stick 'em in the ground, and we'll see," he said mysteriously.

"Don't you know, then?" asked Kate.

"Geneth dda!" grunted Ned. "That's Welsh for wait and see!" And winked at Liz.

Strangely, the more settled in the village they became, the more Liz found herself thinking about London. What was happening to the house? She didn't miss it, or its contents – it had always been more Michael's house than her own. He had been so insistent about the way it should be decorated, whereas she preferred to let a room develop. "No one has white walls any more," he had said, so she lived with elaborate wallpapers she found oppressive. Not worth an argument, though, she had decided. Now she began to worry about it being empty. Perhaps she could contact ask Rodney next door, if the post was still working. Maybe worth a try… just out of curiosity.

One evening when Kate in bed, Liz wrote letters. First a brief letter to Rodney, asking for news. Then to an estate agent in the area – No harm in trying, she thought again – and then she wrote to Michael. She kept the letter brief and to the point. "I thought you might like to know that we are in Wales" – he'd know where. "Ben is missing. Can you help? But Kate and I are managing well, since you still send us money. Kate is convinced that Ben will arrive at any moment." Unable to continue, Liz signed off and stuffed the letter in its envelope.

She addressed Rodney's letter, and hoped that the name and borough of the estate agent would be direction enough. She could only think of sending Michael's to his London office; if he wasn't there, perhaps someone would forward it. If he were still alive. She wasn't sure what she felt about him. It was hard to take in her parents being dead, but living in their house surrounded by people who had known them, made them present in a way Michael had never been.

And Ben. She was forgetting the sound of his voice,

and what he looked like, but the outline of him, the way he moved, rather stiff and shy, was imprinted on her mind, as a comfort and a hope.

16

It was a hot and sultry day, as Ben and Alfred neared the village. The sky was getting darker, and the air smelled of rain. Ben was increasingly apprehensive.

"This is it, isn't it?" Alfred asked. "I saw the sign back there. Welsh and English."

"We're practically there," Ben was forced to admit reluctantly. He still had no clear plan. How could he keep Alfred away from his home? How could he distract him? Perhaps he could avoid the village entirely…

But as they turned a corner, there it lay, spread out before them. There was the church, the High Street, and the shining curve of the river. There was their house just in the crook of the river's bend, and the sea in the distance. Seagulls wheeled and shrieked overhead. He stopped to take it in.

Large fat drops of rain started to fall, hiding the tears that rolled down Ben's face.

"What have you stopped for?" said Alfred. "We must be there by now! Look, there's the sea – can't go any further than that! Go on, tell me straight – this is your village, isn't it? Because if it isn't, I'm thinking you've been having me on all this way." He stepped closer to Ben, and grabbed him.

"All right, all right!" Ben sniffed, tried to shrug him off. "Yes, it's my village – I was just going to tell you!"

"So where's this famous house of yours, then?" Alfred asked.

"Guess!" said Ben.

Alfred twisted Ben's arm behind his back. "Don't you play games with me, little boy! Come on – out with it!"

"It's further on," Ben lied. "Nearer the sea." An idea began to form. It might work as long as nobody recognised him. Always supposing there's anyone left, he thought. Ben dragged his anorak out of the rucksack, put it on, pulled the hood up, and drew the front over his forehead.

"Afraid of a bit of rain?" jeered Alfred, turning up his jacket collar, his feet fidgeting with impatience.

"We might be taken for Runners," Ben said. "They could set the Cleaners on us."

"But they'll know you – they'll think I'm your mate, won't they?"

"Might," replied Ben. If someone saw him and knew him, he couldn't lead Alfred past his house, to – well, somewhere else. If they were stopped as Runners, both of them were in trouble: Ben could show them where he lived, but then Alfred would know where the house was.

"No one's going to stop us – come on." Alfred strode on down the hill. "It is this way, isn't it?" he asked.

Ben nodded.

There was no one about. It was late afternoon and now the rain was teeming – who would be out in such weather? But that only makes us more obvious, Ben thought. So much for sneaking into the village. Ben tugged Alfred out of the way of a car that sent up a wave. They were both drenched.

"Fucking hell!" Alfred moaned. "We'd better be there soon, or we're going to be catch our deaths!"

Ben giggled.

"What? What's the matter?" said Alfred.

"Catching our deaths!" said Ben, now shaking with hysterical laughter. "We spend all that time nose to nose with the disease, and bodies, and sick people – and you're bothered about catching cold!" His laughter turned to coughing as he inhaled rain.

"See? What did I say?" said Alfred. "Now, where do we go?"

"Straight on," said Ben, calming down. They were nearing a wall that Ben knew well – he'd spent lots of time climbing up it and over it. He resisted the desire to gaze up at his garden. As they passed their front gate, he glimpsed the car. They got here! he thought, with immense relief. He and sighed shakily. Alfred squinted at him suspiciously but said nothing.

They went on down the road.

"Where can I take him? Which house can I use? How can I get away?" Ben asked himself as they plodded on.

Many houses they passed were familiar to Ben now: holiday homes, traditional stone cottages, and a few solid nineteen-thirties places. Then came fields, and finally, dunes and the sea. He didn't want to go as far as that. He needed to find something that would impress Alfred.

Then he remembered the very place. "Not far now," he said encouragingly.

"Better not be," said Alfred. "I'm sick of all this!"

After a few more twists and turns of the road – "We going all the way to the beach?" Alfred asked irritably – and Ben turned sharply to the right onto a narrow driveway. "This'll lead us to the beach, won't it?" asked Alfred warily. "Or at least the mouth of the river."

"Yeah, that's right," answered Ben. "But this takes us to the house, see – the garden backs on to the river." He led Alfred along the driveway, glancing round corners, praying no one would spring out on them.

They rounded the final bend to the house, a huge late-Victorian edifice with little pointed turrets and towers, terracotta plaques, and wrought-iron finials.

"Cor!" breathed Alfred, creeping up to peer through the windows.

Ben sighed. It was, as he'd remembered, a pretty splendid affair – as long as it was empty. He looked round. No sign of any vehicles. Ben had heard tales about this house – how the owner's boyfriend had committed suicide, and the owner – Mr. Shelby? Shalby? – had walked away abandoning everything inside just as it as it was. People in the village had talked about it all that summer, not that Ben had understood when he was young, but the house was still both fascinating and frightening.

"Family not here, then? What did I tell you? Anything could have happened to them. So, we going in, then?" asked Alfred.

"Thought you'd like to look round outside, first," said Ben. "The back garden overlooks the river, and there's a boat, and everything."

"I don't want to buy it, I told you," Alfred growled. "Oh, okay – go on, then," he said, seeing Ben's face fall. Ben wasn't sure what to do next. It all came back to the same problem: losing Alfred.

Alfred was enjoying himself now, looking through the windows, and gazing at the view, exactly like a prospective buyer. "You got some amazing stuff!" he remarked. "What say we go in and get dry now? Find ourselves something to eat and drink, eh? Got a key, then?" he added, as Ben hesitated.

"No," said Ben. He was gambling, hoping this house would be like his, or others he knew – there'd be a useful key tucked away in an obvious place, like… Ben tipped the flowerpot next to the back door. Nothing. He ran his hand across the ledge above the door. Nothing. There was an ornamental stone frog near the door; he felt underneath it and in its mouth. Nothing. He was about to check the water butt when he heard the crash of glass.

Alfred appeared round the corner of the house, looking pleased with himself. "All you need is a bit of brute force!" he said.

"What if someone heard you?" said Ben, appalled.

"Thought you said it was empty!"

"I didn't say anything about…"

Alfred dragged him round the corner to face a narrow, broken window. "Leads into the hall. Take your jacket off!"

"What for?" Ben began.

Alfred snatched the anorak, and wrapped it round his fist to bash out the remaining shards of glass. "Now get that flowerpot," he commanded.

Ben obediently lugged the pot to the window, and watched as Alfred upended it. "Right," said Alfred. "Stand on here, then you can climb in and open the door. You're smaller than me."

Ben climbed in, slid to the floor, overbalanced and cut the base of his thumb on a piece of the broken glass. "Fuck, fuck, fuck!" he breathed. There seemed to be a lot of blood, and it hurt.

Alfred was banging at the back door. "Come on! What are you up to? Fucking let me in!" he was calling.

Ben went along the passage and unbolted the back door.

"Took your time!"

"Cut my hand," said Ben.

"Don't show me – can't stand the sight of blood!"

"But you don't mind dead bodies?"

"Course not – no blood." Alfred stepped inside, and glanced round. "You sure there's no one here?"

"What do you think, after all that row? If my Mum

was here, she'd have come running," said Ben, crossly. The strange house smelt damp and closed-in. It felt wrong to be there.

"Give it the once-over?" asked Alfred. "Never know who might have got in while you've been away." He, too, seemed jumpy. "Lead on – it's your house!"

Ben moved along the hallway. Scullery, kitchen, breakfast room at the back, then a grand dining-room and "Telly room?" asked Alfred.

"Yeah," shrugged Ben. It was a bit like the sitting-room in London, with what his father called "Art" on the walls, and uncomfortable-looking antique furniture.

"Must be worth a fortune!" said Alfred.

"Only if you can sell it," Ben retorted.

"Know what he paid for it, your old man?"

"No idea," said Ben.

They tiptoed up the wide stairs, though the carpet was thick enough to deaden any noise. Bedrooms, bathrooms, and attics – they checked them all. All were empty, dusty, and stuffy with disuse. Then they hurried back down to the kitchen, grabbing musty towels from the downstairs cloakroom to dry the rain that still dripped from their hair and faces.

"Where's she keep the food, your mum?" asked Alfred, pulling open doors and drawers. "Fridge's empty."

"Of course it is," said Ben scornfully. "You never leave stuff in the fridge when you're away."

"Clever, aren't you? So where's the food, then? You should know!"

Ben opened a door in the corner of the kitchen: the larder, a large, shelf-lined cupboard, stacked with jars and tins, and packets of pasta, beans, rice, cous-cous… just the way his mother used to stock her store cupboard. "Here," Ben announced, "What do you fancy?"

Alfred browsed the contents, then chose a tin of boeuf Bourguignon, a partly used jambon de Bayonne that hung from a hook, a jar of pork rillettes, a tinned Polish hunters' stew with sausages, and some bottled artichoke hearts.

"I thought you were vegetarian," said Ben.

"Not when I can get meat," Alfred replied. "And this is class stuff – straight from the deli! Where's the tin-opener? – Magic!" he crowed, spotting an electric one on the wall. "You get the plates and knives and forks, and I'll do the rest."

But there was no electricity. Ben remembered the old bull's head tin opener he had in his rucksack and pulled it out. He really didn't want Alfred asking where his mother kept the spare tin-opener.

Alfred, unimpressed and swearing, hacked open tins while Ben searched for cutlery and plates. He opened drawers and cupboards at random, found glasses, mugs, a tea-set, cake-stands, shelves full of expensive-looking kitchen equipment – blender, juicer, sandwich-maker, and several shiny anonymous machines.

"What the fuck are you playing at?" said Alfred, who was watching him. "Don't you know where she keeps stuff?"

Ben mumbled, "Haven't been here for years." He slammed a few more drawers and cupboards open, and finally found some crockery.

Alfred, who had opened all his tins and jars, gestured towards a drawer in the kitchen table. Cutlery. "That's where we keep it at the farm, right? Seems obvious."

Ben put out a bowl and a plate each, while Alfred sorted knives and forks. He also put out a large, serious-looking carving knife. "For the ham," Alfred said. "You having some? You get to choose first, seeing as it's your house. Isn't it?"

"I got you here, didn't I?" Ben replied after a pause.

Alfred shrugged, and started eating out of a tin. "Yeah, you did," he said through a mouthful of cold stew.

Ben started to shave thin slices off the ham with the carving knife, then decided it looked too dead. He ate some artichokes, forking them out of the jar, and a sausage from the Polish stew, and stopped, full.

Alfred was still eating – and drinking. At the bottom of the larder he'd found some dusty bottles, labelled "Parsnip", "Dandelion" and "Blackberrry" in faded copperplate writing.

"You'd think they'd have some proper drink in a place like this!" he had said in disgust. Ben knew the "proper drink" would be in a cabinet of some kind in the living-room, but chose not to say this, Alfred was undeterred by the labels. He opened the "Dandelion" and took a swig. "Not bad!" he said, swilling the liquid round his mouth, before gulping and taking more.

"Have some," he said generously, thrusting the bottle in Ben's direction.

"I'm all right, thanks," said Ben.

Alfred went on drinking and shovelling in beef, pork and shreds of ham. "Chewy," he muttered, but kept eating. He was used to Ben not eating, but not drinking bothered him. "Come on," he wheedled. "Just a sip, go on!"

Ben took the bottle and sipped.

"More!" said Alfred, upending the bottle into Ben's mouth. "We'll open that blackberry one next. That'll be just like Ribena." He wrenched the cork out with his teeth, and courteously passed the bottle to Ben. Ben sipped again. It was rather good – sweet and almost perfumed, with a delicious warmth that started in his stomach and spread. He took another sip, and then gulped a mouthful down. The warmth increased pleasantly. His cut hand didn't hurt so much. He was about to swig again, when Alfred wrested the bottle from him. "Share and share alike!" he said, before drinking half the bottle in one go.

"Mine!" said Ben, snatching the bottle back. "My house, my drinks…" He giggled. He felt in control and clever. He took another gulp. He looked sideways at Alfred, who had found another bottle. "Smine," Ben said. "Gimme!"

Alfred took a long drink, then spluttered. "Stronger than the pink one," he said, offering it to Ben.

Ben, wiser now, took several small sips, then gulped. "That's how to do it!" he said, shaking the bottle at Alfred.

"I think you're getting pissed!" said Alfred, woozily. "Me, too! Time we went to bed – come on, boy. Show me the bedroom."

Ben stood up. The room swung and his head was spinning. His feet seemed to belong to someone else.

"Come on, beddy-byes!" Alfred pushed Ben out of the kitchen and along the hall. They staggered up the stairs to the first floor, Ben pulling himself up by the bannister. "You won't be happy in the morning," Alfred jeered. "Now, where do I sleep?"

Ben pushed open the nearest door. It looked like the master bedroom; he glimpsed a bathroom through an open door. "You can go in here," he said. "It's the best room."

"Okay," said Alfred. "It'll do. Now, show me where your room is."

"Oh, it's upstairs," he said.

"Course it is," said Alfred. "Show me – I'd like to see the little boy's room. And I want to know where you'll be!" He grasped Ben's arm, and drew him up the next flight, yanking him onwards when Ben stumbled. "Right," he said, as they faced three doors. "Which one is yours?"

"Doesn't matter," said Ben indistinctly, "any one! Who cares?"

"I do." And Alfred gave Ben a shake and a shove towards the nearest door.

Ben opened the door a crack, and shut it quickly.

"Well?" asked Alfred.

"No," said Ben. "Not mine."

He flung the door wide to a room decked in flowery pink, with a flounced dressing-table.

"I should hope not!" said Alfred, laughing thickly. "Try again!"

Ben tried another door. "This is mine," he said. This room was decorated in pale blue, with gauzy frilled curtains and many little china ornaments dotted about its surfaces. "My Mum did it for me," Ben insisted. He blundered on. "She thought I'd like it…"

"She's got funny ideas, your mum," said Alfred. Then he pushed open the third door, revealing a thin slip of a room full of books, with photographs of Greek statues on the walls, and a narrow sofa bed.

"Of couse, this is my room, really," said Ben, improvising through increasing drunken haziness. "You see, I didn't want my mum to know I didn't like the other room, so I pretended to use it , and slept in here…" He slurred to a halt.

"With all your books," said Alfred.

"Yes," said Ben.

Alfred pulled out a book. "Robert Mapplethorpe? Gore Vidal? You gay, or what?"

"No!" said Ben, louder than he'd intended – an image of the man in the car reared up, so vivid that he retched.

To Ben's horror, Alfred began to giggle. "All right, keep your hair on – and your trousers, and your little knick-knacks – think I care? I could have you any time, if I'd wanted, right?" He threw the books onto the floor, and flung an arm round Ben.

"Gerroff!" Ben struggled giddily.

"And it's not even your house, is it?" Alfred breathed drunkenly into his ear. "I saw – I saw you! Didn't know where things were kept – don't know your own room – you cheated me, little posh boy. After all I did for you…!"

"No!" Ben wriggled and fought. "Anyway it's a better house than mine – way more stuff…"

"Not the point, posho! You told me lies. Did I ever lie to you?"

Ben was sure he had, but was too drunk to remember. "All the time," he mumbled.

Alfred grabbed Ben by both arms, managing to knock Ben's cut as he did so. Ben cried out in pain, and tried to twist out of Alfred's grip. Alfred held him firmly, and his face, too close to Ben's, was distorted with rage. As they scuffled together, swaying dangerously near the top of the stairs, Ben kneed Alfred sharply in the groin. As Alfred doubled up, Ben clung onto the bannister, and kicked Alfred's back as hard as he could with wobbly legs. Alfred toppled down the stairs until he came to rest with a loud crack as his head hit the bottom corner of the newel post.

Ben shut his eyes and gripped the banister. The dizziness was worse. He opened his eyes, and there was Alfred, still and quiet on the landing. His neck seemed to be at a curious angle. Ben blinked. Alfred was still there. Not moving.

Part of Ben wanted to poke Alfred hard, and shout, "What the fuck are you playing at?" Another part of him couldn't bear to go anywhere near… Was he still breathing? Ben's vision was too blurred, and he couldn't stand up much longer. He lurched towards the room he'd claimed as his and lay down. His head spun. He hauled himself to the window, opened it and was violently sick. He hung onto the sill for a while, breathing the fresh damp air.

What now? He'd probably killed Alfred. He'd seen hundreds of bodies, but he hadn't known any of them. He couldn't bring himself to go near Alfred's body. He turned back to the room, and went to curl up on the sofa. Home. He was so near, he could just walk away. But Alfred…

He woke up thirsty, with a rough throat and sticky mouth. It took him a while to remember where he was. His head hurt, and so did his hand. Then it all came back – the strangers' house, the food, the drink… Oh, god – Alfred!

He dragged himself up from the sofa, head pounding. Alfred.

Ben walked to the door, and peered out. No sounds.

He looked over the bannister rail to where the … but there was no body, no Alfred with his neck askew. Must have been a dream, then – surely?

Ben crept down the stairs to the landing where he had seen Alfred hit his head. For a dream his memory was remarkably clear. He looked for blood. None. He edged down the next flight of stairs and poked his head round the door of the master bedroom. Perhaps he hadn't killed him – perhaps he'd just gone to his room to sleep. But no sign. The bed wasn't even rumpled. He tiptoed cautiously, as he hearkened for the slightest sound – the creak of the stairs, the thump of his heart.

Perhaps he hadn't killed him. He headed for the kitchen. So where was he? It couldn't have been a dream – the details were too vivid – the knee, the kick, the crack of the head…

The evidence of their feast was before him – empty tins and jars, dirty plates and cutlery, and the ham… The carving knife had been speared into the ham with such force that it was pinned to the table. He didn't want to eat. A bottle rolled back and forth on its side across the table – chink, chink – and somewhere a door slammed. Ben started. Alfred? There was a breeze… Gathering his courage, Ben went into the hall. The front door was wide open, and the house felt empty. Ben went outside, and slammed the door shut behind him.

17

Liz heard Kate shouting from the front door. Perhaps Mari's early, she thought.

"We've got a letter!" Kate was calling. She waved a thin envelope at Liz. "Can I open it?" she clamoured. "We haven't had one here, before!"

"Who's it addressed to?" Liz asked, calmly enough. "It's probably from the estate agent."

She looked at the crabbed capital letters of the address. For a moment, she half-expected to find a note made of letters cut out from old newspapers, but no, on opening it, was she found Rodney's stiffly joined-up writing.

"Who's it from?" Kate was jumping round her.

"Rodney next door," Liz said. "Now go and play and let me read."

The letter started "Hoping this finds you well. My poor mother recently succumbed..." Liz would have to burn the letter and disinfect her hands, and Kate's. She read on. "The house still looks lived-in, and I have done my best to help, keeping the rubbish from collecting on the front path, and so on. Though the garden at the back is getting a bit wild." Then she gasped. "Had the pleasure of meeting your young man some months back… going to see his grandparents… hope he arrived safely… some activity from police later, but probably nothing…"

Liz was in turmoil. The letter was dated the thirtieth of April. Ben had escaped from school, and been home. For a moment she was euphoric, then she wondered fearfully if the police had taken him. Or was he really on his way to Wales? She couldn't think straight.

She went to find Kate in the garden. "Kate," she began, and then stopped, bursting into tears.

"Wasn't it a nice letter?" Kate asked.

"I don't know," she said, trying to sound cheerful. "Rodney says that he saw Ben at home – he's got away from school!"

"Told you!" Kate said, returning to her game.

Since Rodney's letter, Liz's feelings had swung from one extreme to another. Ben was on his way. Kate was sure of that, and sometimes Liz was, too. But when she tried to work out how long it took to walk from London to Cardigan, and thought of the dangers on the way, she had to busy herself in the garden, digging and weeding, to calm down… She couldn't leave the problem alone: three hundred-odd miles, at a rate of, say, two-and-a-half to three miles an hour… Ten miles a day, maybe? She had to get pencil and paper. By her calculations, he could have been here in only three days since Rodney saw him, and that would have been weeks ago. But, she reminded herself, he had to sleep, and find food, perhaps work... She wished she hadn't started to look so closely at the reality of the situation. She wished she was like Kate, who was immersed in her Welsh lessons, her stories, and her patch of garden, and her unshakeable belief that Ben was going to appear at any minute. Kate also kept Ben's bedroom in a state of well-dusted readiness.

"You wouldn't like to dust the sitting-room, I suppose?" Liz asked.

"No," Kate replied. "I just thought his room ought to be nice for him."

"And the sitting-room ought to be nice for us," said Liz.

Kate shrugged, and went to deliver a new episode of her story to Mrs. Phillips.

"And don't stay too long," Liz called after her.

Liz was constantly occupied, apart from in the garden. Food was now in short supply; she had to be imaginative to stretch her ingredients. Meat and fish, and even vegetables, had to be eked out with rice or pasta. When Mari came for Welsh conversation, she told Liz if Cyril up the road, or the supermarket in town, had rice or pasta, or loo roll, or washing-up liquid.

"Don't need to waste your money on washing-up liquid," said Auntie Rye. "Hot water and bicarb'll do the job. That and elbow grease!"

Liz felt she'd been spoilt all her life. She didn't dare mention the lack of cleaning sprays or J-cloths, but set about finding old towels to cut up and hem. The sewing was calming. She got more adventurous and started to renovate some of the older sheets by cutting them down their thin middles and rejoining them at their edges, as her mother had done.

"Are you making a ghost costume?" Kate asked.

When Liz explained the process, Kate went quiet for a moment. "Are we very poor, then?" she asked.

"No, not really," Liz said. "But the whole country is running out of... things," she said.

"Why?" Kate asked, reasonably enough.

Liz took a deep breath. She had to be honest. "Because of the sickness," she said. "People keep dying, so there aren't enough people left making things, and delivering stuff round the country. So the more we can learn to do for ourselves, the better."

Kate sat down next to Liz and leaned up against her. "Like television?" she asked at last.

"Well, we can't do that! But we can keep telling stories, and singing..."

"Not as good as cartoons!" Kate said. "And I don't want to sleep on a sheet with a bump down the middle! I liked it best before," she whined. "I want to go back to London, and school, and the old house... Don't want to keep – pretending!" she burst out.

Liz was shocked. "Pretending what?" she asked.

"That everything's all right, and normal, like we're on holiday. We're not! Everything's all muddled, and you don't know where Daddy is, and Ben's not here yet..."

She began to howl, pushing her head into Liz's lap.

"I know," said Liz. "I know..." She rocked the sobbing child until her tears finally stopped. "It's new, and it's difficult – it's not going to be lovely all the time."

"It's never lovely!" Kate started to cry again.

"It is sometimes," Liz insisted. "Look how we've made new friends – look how good your Welsh is getting, and your writing – remember how difficult you found it? And now you write wonderful stories... and you grow things in the garden – we're having one of your lettuces tonight – and you're beginning to be a good at cooking, too..."

Kate rubbed her wet face on her sleeve. "And it's raining," she said in tragically.

Liz started to laugh. "Well, I can do a lot of things, but I can't control the weather!"

Kate began to giggle. "Why not? You're no use!" She pushed her mother away. "I want television and I want sun. And Ben," she announced.

"I want Ben, and I want a garden full of healthy vegetables, and..." She ran out of ideas, and grabbed Kate and started tickling her. Kate screamed in delight and fell off the sofa. "And I want you to laugh a lot," Liz ended, pulling Kate back onto her lap.

"I will, I will," said Kate into her mother's neck.

"Let's go and make some lunch," said Liz. "I'm hungry."

As they were looking through the fridge for sandwich material – "Bacon," said Kate; "Tomatoes," said Liz, and started cutting bread – there was an insistent knocking at the door. Kate ran to answer, and Mrs. Phillips appeared in the kitchen.

"Do join us," said Liz, pleased to see another adult.

"Oh, I don't want to bother you, but I do need a quick word."

Something in her demeanour warned Liz that Kate might be better occupied elsewhere. "Why don't you go and finish your story for Mrs. Phillips? I'll call you when lunch is ready." She heard Kate go to the sitting-room and opening the desk to find her work. "Don't rush – there's plenty of time," she called. "Now," she said.

"I don't want to worry you," Mrs Phillips began, pulling out a chair, "but there seem to have been some odd people hanging about recently. I'm not the only one to have noticed, either – Mari was telling me the other day… and Ned, too…"

"What sort of people?" Liz interrupted.

"Well, they seemed… older than your boy, and they were looking at your house, a girl and a young man – the man seemed to be injured – arm in a sling, you know. They didn't seem to be the sort of people you'd know, so I thought I'd mention it."

She was irked at the presumption there were people she should or shouldn't know. Still, who would watch her house? Someone with a message from Ben? Why wouldn't he get in touch directly? Unless he was… She put her head in her hands.

"I'm sorry," Mrs. Phillips's voice was kind and

troubled. "Maybe they were just 'casing the joint'" – Mrs. Phillips spoke in italics, and tried to smile. "There have been a lot of robberies recently – empty houses, holiday homes, and so on. People talk about it. And not enough police, of course…"

"You were right to tell me," Liz said at last. "There's nothing much I can do if anyone wants to rob me, but supposing there's a message…"

"If there's a message, I don't see why the buggers couldn't come to the front door, like normal people!" said Mrs. Phillips in her usual brusque tone. "But then I suppose I don't know what's normal any more. But if you find yourself in any difficulty… well, I do still have my husband's old Army pistol tucked away…"

"Oh, no!" Liz was shocked. "It wouldn't come to that, surely?

"You never know what you can do until you're tested." Mrs. Phillips sounded so earnest that Liz wanted to giggle. She remembered how she'd felt when Mari lost Kate: anything was possible.

"Come on, let's eat," said Liz, and called Kate. "And you are staying for lunch, aren't you?" she said, daring Mrs. Phillips to refuse.

They sat together round the kitchen table, Kate chattering away about the next instalment of her story. Mrs. Phillips responded courteously as always. Liz hardly said a word. Neither adult ate with any appetite.

"I'm going in the garden," Kate announced when she had finished her sandwich.

"Wait a moment, and I'll come with you – we can do a bit of work together," said Liz.

"And I'm going home to get on with things," said Mrs. Phillips, putting their plates in the sink, and picking up Kate's story.

"I'm only going to play. You don't have to come," Kate said to her mother.

"Thought you'd like a bit of company," said Liz.

"No," said Kate. "I want to play by myself. I'm sick of gardening."

"Well, I'll garden, and you can play," said Liz reasonably.

"It's not the same when you're hanging about watching me," Kate said crossly.

"I promise not to look at you!" Liz said, in mock supplication, but Kate had gone.

She began to wash up the lunch things, still resolved to follow her outside.

She was just stacking the plates in the drainer, when Kate appeared at the back door. "That was quick!" Kate leant against the doorpost. Her face was white. "What's the matter?" Liz demanded. "What's happened?"

"Nothing!" Kate whispered.

"But why…?"

"Nothing!" said Kate, more emphatically.

Liz was cold with fear, but "If you won't tell me, you'll have to show me," and with more courage than she felt, stretched out her hand to Kate, and moved towards the garden.

"No!" Kate shouted, flinging her arms round her mother's waist. "There's noises out there – in the shed! I don't want to go!"

"You stay here, then," said Liz. "I'll go and look. I expect it's just mice. Or a hedgehog."

"Bigger," said Kate. "Don't go!"

Liz shook Kate off. If there are strangers hanging about, it's better to confront them, she thought. Kate rushed to the sitting-room and buried her head under the cushions. "It'll be all right!" Liz called. "I'll be right back."

She went through the front door, round the side of the house, and up the uneven steps to the garden, where she paused. The air smelled fresh and clean after the rain; the garden glittered, grass and leaves hung with raindrops. Everything seemed peaceful. She looked across the garden to the shed. No point in rushing into trouble. Then she heard a scritching-scratching sound – animals, of course. The shed door was shaking, as though something were trying to get out. It must have swollen shut in the wet.

The door burst open.

A tall skinny silhouette appeared, stumbling slightly from the effort of forcing the door. The figure stood very still, and Liz saw that he was dirty and thin, and his clothes were in tatters.

"It's all right," Liz called, "I won't hurt you!"

The figure leaned against the shed wall for a moment, shaking. Then Liz saw that he was crying – or laughing...

"What's the matter?" she asked, stepping nearer.

A small fierce person pushed Liz out of the way. Liz saw Kate rush up to the stranger and fling her arms round him. "I told you!" she was yelling. "I told you he was coming!"

"Get her off me!" came a familiar voice, deeper than she remembered. "She's hurting my hand! Mum!"

"Ben?" She ran across the wet grass to him, and stopped. "Let him go!" she said to Kate He was taller and dirtier and somehow older, and he was struggling to release himself from Kate's clutches.

She reached out to hug him.

"Ben!" She tried not to cry. She was close enough to touch him now; she patted him on the back, edging him towards the house. She could smell the sourness of him. "Come on, my love," she murmured.

Why hadn't he come to the house? Where had he been all this time?

"Whatever were you doing in the shed?" she asked.

"It was raining," Ben said.

"It's been raining lots," Kate chattered, bouncing round him. "And we haven't even been to the beach yet, and Mummy said we could go when you came – "

"Come inside, both of you," Liz said.

"Right!" she said once they were inside. "Kate, for goodness' sake, let him go! And Ben…!"

She watched as he looked round the kitchen, as if he were checking that everything was still the same. She wanted to grab him, to feel the thin bony shoulders and stroke his rough hair. Ben backed away.

"Can I have a bath?" he asked.

His words made no sense for a moment.

"Bath – of course you can have a bath! There're clean clothes in your bedroom. And I'll make…" Her voice trailed away… "supper!" she said. It was much too early for supper.

Both children disappeared upstairs, Ben plodding heavily, as if he carried a great weight.

Later, checking Ben's bed was made up, she heard taps running and splashing from the bathroom, and saw Kate sitting with her back against the bathroom door, chatting – "And that's when I started working with Mrs. Phillips… town with Mari, and these kids… just like a gnome, and there's lots of…" Liz heard an occasional grunt from behind the door; Ben was listening to some of it.

She returned to finish the preparations for supper. When had he last eaten a proper meal?

At last he and Kate came down to the kitchen. Ben was wearing jeans that didn't reach his ankles, but still sagged at the waist, and an old sweatshirt that Liz wore for gardening.

"We'll have to kit you out!" said Liz, hoping for a smile that didn't appear.

Kate was still excited. "Do you want to read my stories?" she was saying. "I've done lots and lots!"

"Okay," Ben said, and watched while Kate sped off to fetch them.

"So?" Liz said. Where to begin? Should she start asking him about his journey? Or should she let him talk when he was ready? She looked at his dear face. Still Ben, but with a new distant, strained look about him.

"So what?" he said with a twitch of a smile. "I'm here, aren't I? And I'm clean. And I went in the shed because it was raining. And it seemed too soon to…"

"To what?" Liz asked.

"To come in and go through all the questions – the stories! It's been a long time. And it's not over."

He sounded so sad. Liz moved towards him, arms out. He shuffled back, to lean against the doorpost.

Liz let her arms fall to her sides. Too soon. "So what's not over?" she asked.

"Oh… stuff…" he said, shaking his head.

Liz shrugged. "Are you hungry?" she asked. "Because I'm doing roast vegetables with pasta, and then –

"No!" he said. "No, thank you. We ate last night."

"We," Liz noted. "Okay," she said "But you'll sit with us when we eat later, won't you?"

"Maybe," he said. "I'll go up to my room, now – I'm tired."

"But you were going to read my stories," Kate wailed, returning with an untidy pile of paper.

"Later," he said.

"Let him be," said Liz. "He needs to recover a bit."

"But what's the matter with him?" Kate said. "He's home now."

"He's just tired, I expect."

"You used to say that about Daddy!" She flounced off to sulk in her newest tent.

Ben was home, but Liz felt, strangely, that they were still waiting. Now and then she told herself that everything was fine. It wasn't. Ben joined them at meal times but he ate very little. He answered when spoken to, he read to Kate, but part of him was absent: the Ben that discussed things, and worked things out, and worried about being wrong. He spent a lot of time lying on the sofa with a book on his chest, not reading. He tolerated Kate snuggling up to him occasionally and listened to her stories but avoided any contact with his mother.

He can hardly bear to look at me, Liz thought in anguish. Is it because I left him? He wasn't interested in meeting people; every time someone came to the door, he disappeared to his room.

One day at supper, Kate was pushing her food round the plate like Ben did.

"Come on, eat up!" Liz said to Kate, then, "Ben, would you like some more potatoes? You've hardly eaten any – "

Ben stood up and scraped the rest of his dinner into the bin. "I'll eat what I want to!" he said. "And I don't want fucking potatoes, or anything that comes out of the filthy ground!"

"Enough, Ben!" Liz commanded. "I've had enough of this! Tell me what's the matter, or – or – get out of here!" Liz was immediately appalled… That wasn't what she'd meant at all!

"Noooo!" screamed Kate.

Ben sat down and put his head on his arms on the table. His shoulders shook. Kate stroked his back. "There, there," she murmured, glaring at her mother.

"– all I ever thought about," he mumbled. "I thought about you all the time – here – " he sobbed. "And now I've messed it up!"

Liz put her arms round him. "But Ben – it's all we ever thought about, too – and you're here now. It's over!"

"But it isn't!" Ben wailed, lifted his head at last. His voice cracked. "I've done something terrible!"

Liz hugged him and he rested his head on her shoulder. Kate wriggled in between them. For a moment they clung to each other.

"Come on," said Liz. "Let's sit on the sofa, and hear all about it."

"I can't…" he began. "Not Kate…!"

"Kate, too. Come on," Liz insisted. We're all in this together, she thought, and Kate will take in as much as she can understand. It's best to be open.

Slowly, Ben's story unfolded. Sometimes Liz could follow it; sometimes not. Kate kept asking him to repeat things, like the escape from school. She hid her face in Liz's lap when he told about the man in the car. They enjoyed the more peaceful episode in Rufus's wood. Then the Chocolate farm. Liz held both children very close while Ben told them. Behind his matter-of-fact narration, Liz could hear his fear and horror, and marvelled at her son's courage and sense of purpose.

"You did so well," she said.

"No!" Ben jerked free. "I didn't escape…!"

"But you're here now," said Kate, her face crumpled with tears.

Ben went on to complete the story – walking past their house with Alfred; breaking in to the place down the road; the food, the drink, the fight. "… and I was sure he was dead, but when I woke up he was gone!" he ended.

"Then you can't have killed him," said Liz calmly.

Ben got up and paced the sitting-room, touching the furniture as he went. "If he's alive he'll come and find me. He'll want me back on the farm – they didn't get their money's-worth."

"I saw him," said Kate in a small voice.

Ben and Liz turned.

"But why didn't you…?"

"What?"

"I was in the garden" said Kate. "I didn't know who they were – the man had his arm tied up in a scarf, and the girl had a white hat, well, not really white… They were looking at all the houses…"

Liz and Ben exchanged looks for the first time since Ben's return.

"Megan's come," said Ben.

"See? He is alive. Megan probably helped him get away from the house."

"But how did she get here? And now they're both looking for me," said Ben.

"We won't let them get you!" said Kate, clutching Ben's hand so that he winced.

"That's my bad hand!" he said.

"Let me see," said Liz, taking his arm. Then, "Kate – will you go and find Mrs. Phillips?" It was the first time she had got close enough to Ben to see the wound; it was red and puffy and oozing slightly. "Not good," she said.

"I don't want to see anyone," Ben said.

"Mrs. Phillips was a nurse," said Liz.

"Yeah… right. So was Megan."

18

Liz was soon used to seeing Ben's new tall frame lounging about the house, Kate trailing after him like a needy puppy. Sometimes, Liz invented things to do – "Just you and me, Kate," – so that Ben had some time alone. That way, Kate had some undivided attention, and Ben had some breathing space.

Gardening and cooking took up most of the daytime. In the evenings, they listened to the radio. They sat through "Kate's Music Night", where Kate chose favourite tapes from her grandfather's collection, and they sang together, even Ben.

When Kate was in bed, Liz and Ben talked about their future: how bad supplies would get, whether the gas and electricity would run out – this terrified Liz until Ben mentioned Rufus's oil lamps and wood fires. "I know how to grow stuff as well," Ben added, wryly.

They seldom went out. Liz didn't like to leave them alone, but occasionally popped up to Cyril's, to see what he had in. Local fishermen and farmers were beginning to bring him supplies, now that supermarket suppliers were no longer interested: it wasn't worth their while to travel and freeze goods. Sometimes she returned with a piece of Welsh lamb, or a gurnard or plaice. It was expensive, but at least Ben would eat fish and meat. Friends helped, too. Mrs. Phillips went to the market on her old bike, and brought back tea, cheese and bacon in its capacious basket. Auntie Rye would turn up with Ned's huge runner beans or peas. Mari still called in for Kate's Welsh lessons, inviting Ben to join in, but he always disappeared to his room.

"Later, perhaps," Liz said.

No one mentioned Ben's sudden appearance, other than Cyril, who remarked upon an "increase in the family." Liz just smiled.

She worried about Ben. She'd see him peering from behind curtains; he jumped every time anyone came to the door. He went in the garden to help Ned and amuse Kate, but he kept well back from the roadside.

"He'll have gone away by now – and the girl," Liz tried to reassure him.

"You don't know what he's like!" Ben said.

Rumours of strangers still circulated; Mari was especially keen to warn them. "We have to look out for our own," she said, gloomily.

As the days went by and nothing happened, Ben became less jumpy. He was eating more, and had stopped picking bits of carrot or potato out of his food.

"Ben looked right over the fence and up and down the road," Kate reported one day.

"Did you see anything?" Liz asked.

Ben shrugged. "Just checking," he said.

"He's gone, Ben," Liz would repeat.

"Yeah…" said Ben.

Liz grew tired of being cooped up. Kate was whingeing about every small task, and Ben was slipping in to idleness.

"We all need more exercise," she said.

"You sound like Nan," said Kate.

"But we can't," said Ben.

"Why not?"

"It's not safe!" Ben raised his voice. "But if you don't care…!"

"Of course we care," Liz said. "We're all safe, now – it's over!"

"Maybe," shrugged Ben.

"Next fine day, we'll go to the beach," Liz said. "OK?"

"Can I come too?" said Kate, in a small voice.

Liz laughed. "Well, we need you to carry the picnic!"

"And the towels," Ben joined in. "The tent. The frying pan –"

"And the buckets and spades," Liz said.

"Kate's been looking forward to going to the beach with you for ages," she told Ben in the kitchen, as they put the last of the picnic together. "It'll be good for all of us to do normal things."

"Day at the beach with little sister sorts everything!" said Ben. "I don't think!"

"It's just a start, Ben," said his mother, so quietly that he felt ashamed.

"Can we make a fire?" he asked, after a while. "Cook bacon, and potatoes maybe?"

"If you can carry it, we can cook it," said Liz.

Ben found food and some matches, and rattled the box. "*Boy's Book of Woodcraft*," he said.

"I think that's in your bedroom – I brought it with us."

"I saw," said Ben. "Rufus wrote bits of it, you know…"

Liz looked at him in amazement. "Really?" she said. "Still some good ones out there, then!"

Liz packed her rucksack with the picnic; Ben lugged the basket with towels and costumes and Kate carried her bucket and spade and a tennis ball. She paused by the car and leaned against it, pleading.

"No good," said Liz. "We just can't use the petrol, Kate. It'll be nice to walk. We might find things."

"What?" said Kate crossly.

"Oh… the first blackberries…? Last strawberries…? Just keep your eyes open!"

Ben led the way; they walked towards the beach, passed the last houses of the village, fields, and then to the dunes.

"I haven't found anything yet," Kate complained. "You said there'd be – "

"I only said might," said Liz. "We're there now – look, there's the lifeboat shop, and the tea-room."

Kate ran on ahead. Both were closed. She turned

back to her mother, looking tragic.

"No treasures," Kate wailed. It was true – the lifeboat shop had sold a curious mixture of second-hand books, shell earrings and necklaces, plastic dragon key rings, notebooks, and pale-leaded pencils. "I wanted to find a present for Nancy."

"Listen," said Liz as gently as she could. "You do know we're not going back to your school in London, don't you? So we won't be seeing Nancy…"

Kate leant against Liz for a moment. "But I could write her a letter, couldn't I?" she said.

"Of course," said Liz. "Come on!" They crossed the rough wooden walkway to the beach.

"'Do not walk barefoot over this walkway.' Look, it's in Welsh underneath, Mummy," Kate read the sign. "Why not?"

"Splinters, silly," said Liz. "Go and catch up with Ben and ask him if he wants rocks or dunes." She could hear Kate yelling questions as she sped off. She saw Ben turn to let Kate catch up, then watched as they became involved in an animated conversation. Both figures traipsed back to her.

"Well?"

"Ben wants rocks and I want dunes," announced Kate.

"Right," said Liz. "I say we make camp at the edge of the dunes, so I can see you both, and after lunch, Ben can go and climb rocks. Okay?"

Ben drew shapes in the sand with a foot.

"Okay," he said. "But first we need to find driftwood for the fire – it takes ages to cook potatoes."

Liz settled herself on the rug that Kate, feeling she had won, had helpfully spread out. "Off you go, then," she said, opening her book.

"Will you be all right by yourself, Mummy?" Kate asked.

"Of course," said Liz stretched out, book in hand, and head on the beach bag. She heard Kate chanting "splinters silly, silly splinters," and then their voices, arguing and teasing, faded into the distance.

She read for a while, then propped herself up against her rucksack so that she had the wide stretch of the beach before her. Away to her right, the mouth of the river sprawled round sandbanks that only locals could negotiate. She had once, as a child, seen sewin caught in nets stretched across a strand of the river. No one knows how to do that any more, she thought sadly. To the left, where the land curved round, there were low cliffs tilting towards the sea, and rock pools that were beginning to fill as the tide crept in. She remembered her Dad taking her to the pools to fish for shrimps, and how they'd taken their catch back home and solemnly boiled all seven of them, to eat for tea with lettuce and salad cream. The children will get used to that sort of thing again – no more takeaways or fish and chips.

Her eyes roamed the beach. Where were they? The tide line was the best place for driftwood. She saw two tiny figures following the shore towards the rocks; they had left a pile of wood out of the tide's reach, and had gone to look further, she supposed.

The sun was warm on her face. She could hear the shush of the long low waves, and the swish of the dune grasses. She could smell the sweet coconut gorse, and the rough salt of the sea. An insect hummed.

She woke suddenly to something tickling her cheek. "Stop it, Kate!" she said, without opening her eyes.

"Wrong one."

"Ben?"

"Wrong again."

She opened her eyes. A figure leant over her, dark against the sun. "Ben! Don't be so silly!" she started, snatching at the long grass in his hand.

Not Ben.

"Alfred?" she guessed, her breathing quickening.

"Right at last!" he said, sitting himself down on the rug. "And you're Mrs. Ben's Mum?"

"I'm Liz Patterson," she said formally. She sat up straight and tucked the rucksack against her side.

"It's all right, you know," said the boy – for he was only a boy. "I don't want your money. Just thought I'd drop by. Talks a lot about you, Ben does. Wanted to see what you were really like. Course, I didn't believe in you to start with – thought he was making you up to get away... And the sister..."

Liz shivered, in spite of the sun. There were no other people in sight, and she didn't want to talk. She suddenly wanted the children back, to go home. But why should she run away from this boy, for god's sake? He was only chatting.

"You all right, there, Liz? I can call you Liz, can't I?"

She shrugged, then said politely, "Thank you so much for bringing Ben home – it was really kind of you. He caused you some sort of accident…?"

"No problem," he said.

"Are you all right now?"

"Oh, it was nothing. I fell down some stairs and knocked myself out. Broke my collarbone, too."

A grubby sling hanging round his neck, not that his arm was in it. "Did you see a doctor?" she asked.

Alfred looked at her, and laughed. "A doctor? Now? Look at me! Anyway, Megan's a nurse."

"Oh," said Liz. "She came with you… and Ben?"

"No – she got a lift, later – worried I was enjoying myself too much!"

"She's here now?" Liz tried to be courteous, though she desperately wanted him to go. "How are you managing? It must be hard to find food and somewhere to stay when you don't know the area."

There was a pause, while Alfred sifted the soft sand through the fingers of his good arm.

"You offering us somewhere, then?" he asked eventually, without meeting her eye.

"Well, no, we haven't got room for visitors, you see…" She wondered why she sounded apologetic. He'd locked Ben up, forced him to do that work… And here he was hanging about, as if there were unfinished business between them. She began to understand Ben's fear.

"You owe me," he went on, without raising his voice. "I looked after your boy – looked out for him. Wouldn't be too much to expect a bit of a thank you, would it?"

I'm the adult here, Liz told herself. She had no idea how to conveyed this to Alfred.

"I have thanked you," Liz said, getting to her feet. "I don't know what else to say. You've managed okay so far?"

She could see the full sweep of the beach again. The little pile of wood was still by the rocks, but there was no sign of either child.

"Can't you see them?" asked Alfred, standing next to her, noting her gaze. "They're probably round by the rocks – want me to go and find them, Liz? I can go faster than you. You don't want that little girl hurt, right?"

"Ben will look after her. Thank you," she said coldly. "I expect you'll want to be getting on. Find your friend – Megan."

"Oh, she's all right. I expect she's making friends with your little girl by now. Fond of kids, Megan is."

"What? Kate's with Ben!"

"All right, she'll be fine! Don't panic. Trained nurse, Megan is – wouldn't hurt a fly!"

Liz was shaking. "Where is she? How do you know she's with Megan?" She should have gone with them, not slept.

She bent down to grab her rucksack. Alfred's foot was on the straps. As she tugged, he moved his foot, and she fell backwards.

"Careful," he said, leaning forward to help her up.

"Get off me!" Liz screamed. "Don't touch me!"

Alfred stood back, hands raised in mock capitulation. "Just trying to help," he said.

"Get the fuck away!" Liz threw the rucksack over her shoulder and started off down the dunes to the beach.

"What about your stuff?" Alfred called.

Liz raised her middle finger, and stumbled towards the dark wet sand, where she started to run. She didn't turn to check if Alfred was following her. She fixed her gaze on the rocks.

The tide was coming in, and the outer layer of rocks was disappearing under curls of foam. There was no danger: larger rocks formed bridges to the cliffs, where there was a path to the road. They had walked it many times. But what if they – especially Kate – were frightened? They might trip, fall in a hurry to get away. She ran on. Her chest hurt, the rucksack banged painfully on her back.

She waded through a shallow stream, stood for a moment on a large flat stone, getting her breath back, and looking round. The sea spilled in, filling the rock pools, and flinging spray into the air. Not a sign of either child. So where…? Even Kate knew you never found driftwood in the rocks. She tried to think where they might have gone, turning to keep all directions in view, expecting to see Ben's lanky form stooping to pick up wood, or Kate, bouncing along behind him. There was the deserted lifeboat shop, and the tea room… no children. No Alfred or Megan. How could they have known that today was their beach day, and that the children would go off searching for driftwood? It wasn't possible. She began to understand what Ben had tried to convey about Alfred: he was a chancer, a storyteller who seized on bits of information, however small, and used them to tease and irritate – and frighten.

Still no children.

She spied a wisp of smoke in the distance. It seemed to rise from the dunes. Was that where she had been sitting? Her footprints on the firm sand were just beginning to disappear in the incoming tide. She followed them back – a thread of hope – along the beach, too tired to run now. As she scrambled up the slipping sand to her camp, she saw Ben, busy with the fire, instructing a sulky Kate.

"Don't put too much wood on yet – we need to get it really red and hot if we want the potatoes to cook."

"Can't we put the sausages on so they'll be ready quickly? I'm starving!"

"No, let's wait till Mum… Mum!" he shouted, seeing her.

"Where were you, Mummy? We were worried!"

"Told you she'd only gone to the loo!"

Liz couldn't speak. We can't stay here – suppose he comes back? she thought. "We ought to go home," she blurted out. "I don't think it's…"

"Look," Ben was saying proudly. "I brought some skewers for the potatoes so they'll cook quicker."

"Wonderful!" said Liz, nearly in tears. "Brilliant! But I thought I'd lost you, and…"

"And I helped with the fire, didn't I, Ben?" said Kate, not listening.

Liz started to rummage in the bags left open on the rug.

"What are you looking for, Mummy? Have we forgotten something?" Kate asked.

"No, no," she replied, grabbing the end of a roll of tinfoil. "Look – you can wrap the potatoes – that should hurry them up a bit." She wasn't sure what she was frightened of. Alfred was unpleasant, maybe threatening, but he hadn't actually done anything. She couldn't explain to them. Ben would understand, but he looked cheerful and busy.

Kate was stripping bark from twigs. "I'm making sausage sticks," she said. "You see, you thread the sausage on and – "

"– and it falls off into the fire!" said Ben.

"It's a good idea," said Liz. "We'll try it!"

Ben and Kate were in charge. They argued cheerfully about when to start the bacon and poked at the potatoes. Liz was too anxious to enjoy the delicious near-charred smell of the meat, the way the smoke spiralled upwards, the little caves of scarlet fire and white ash where the potatoes roasted. The cooking process seemed endless. She was alert to every bird-sound and slippage of sand, but heard only the crackle of the fire and the children's chatter.

The children were stuffing the sausages and bits of

bacon into potato halves to catch the fat. Kate presented her with a half potato. She tried it but couldn't swallow.

"You're not eating your dinner," said Kate self-righteously.

"In a minute," said Liz, wondering how she could dispose of it without offending or worrying the cooks.

"This is good," said Ben. He leant against her back, eating the last potato. Kate quickly nestled up to them.

"Mummy?" said Kate.

"Mmmm?"

"Did you find the loo?"

"Why? Do you want…?"

"No, not now, but when we were looking for wood, I went to the loo at the lifeboat place, and I saw…that girl…"

Liz and Ben stared at Kate. "Who?" Ben asked.

"I don't know her name – the one in the hat I saw with the boy that day…"

"Did she touch you?" Liz said. "Did she speak to you?"

"Of course not!" said Kate. "I don't know her! Anyway, I didn't like her face, so I ran back to Ben."

"You didn't tell me," said Ben.

"I'm telling you now, aren't I?" said Kate reasonably. "She doesn't matter, anyway."

"So why are you talking about her?" Ben asked.

"She just came into my head. Oh, and when we came back here with the wood, I saw them both snuggled up in a dune, over there." Kate waved a hand vaguely.

"You should have said," Ben said, tight-lipped.

"I think we ought to pack up," said Liz, "Hurry up, you two!"

Kate didn't protest. They agreed who carried what, and set off across the open beach towards the walkway.

"You all right with that, Kate?" asked Liz. "I can put the rug in the picnic bag if you like."

Kate, pink and tired from sun, staggered under the rug rolled over her shoulders.

"I'll take it," said Ben, and grabbed it from her.

"I can do it!" she retorted.

"But I can do it better!"

Kate stomped on ahead, swinging her bucket crossly. "And we didn't even swim!" she shouted back over her shoulder.

"Next time," said Liz. "Another day…" She stopped. Kate had arrived at the walkway, and she stopped too.

Someone was standing by the fence that ran along the walkway's sandy boards.

19

"Frighten you, did I?" said a voice." Wouldn't hurt a fly, me – I'm a nurse. Till I got sick, of course."

Now Ben stopped. "What do you want, Megan?" he asked.

She gave no answer, but moved aside to let them pass.

At the other end, by the road, was another figure.

"Hallo, Liz," it said. "Everything all right, then?"

"What are you doing here?" Ben asked, his voice cracking.

"Same as you – enjoying the weather. Don't own the beach, do you? I've been introducing myself to your dear Mummy, haven't I, Liz?"

Ben looked at his mother, who nodded.

"We did meet," she said.

"You didn't tell me," Ben said.

"It wasn't important," Liz said.

"We had a nice little chat," Alfred went on, as though no one else had spoken. "Agreed that you owe me, Ben – you haven't worked your contract out."

"I didn't have a contract!" Ben exclaimed.

Kate clung to Liz's arm.

"Well, more a sort of… gentleman's agreement…?"

"No contract," Megan said suddenly. "Food."

"But I was working for you…!" Ben yelled.

"Stop this nonsense!" shouted Liz.

"That's right, Liz – you tell him!" Alfred smirked.

"This is stupid!" Liz looked at both boys, one wrapped in the rolled picnic rug, and the other doing a strange little side-to-side dance. Megan slid round to stand near Alfred. Kate held fast to Liz. "Now look," Liz said. "All this rubbish – it's got to stop. We don't owe you anything. Ben doesn't work for you, and he's not going to, either."

"Food," muttered Megan.

"Well, if you hadn't fed him, he wouldn't have been able to work, would he? And you obviously managed fine before he came. You need to go back to your farm, and get on with your work there."

"Yes," said Megan. "Home, Alfred. I want to go home."

"Who cares what you want! You can't tell me what to do!" Alfred turned on Megan so viciously that she recoiled from him. "Who does all the work, anyway? Who makes all the decisions, eh? And who decided to take on Ben? Me, that's who! You're just stupid!"

Megan's hard little face collapsed into tears.

"There's no need for that," Liz remonstrated. "I'm sure she does her best."

"Her best isn't worth a fly!" Alfred snarled.

"Wouldn't hurt…" Megan was sobbing. "Nurse, that's me…"

"See?" Alfred said. "She ain't got the sense she was born with. That's why I took up with Ben, here – I can train him."

"He belongs with his family," insisted Liz. Kate was shaking her arm. "What? What's the matter?"

"Look! Megan's running away!"

They all turned; Megan was stumbling up the cliff path.

"Come back, you silly bint!" Alfred shouted. He turned to the others. "I told you she was daft – she's going the wrong way if she thinks she's off home by herself! Megan!" he yelled.

"Get her," Ben said to Alfred. "It's not safe up there."

"Don't you start! What's it got to do with you? She can look after herself."

"You said she was stupid just now," Ben retorted.

"You go and get her if you're so stuck on her!"

Ben stared at Alfred, as if willing him to move. Then he took all their beach things, and arranged them in a pile at the edge of the walkway. "See you in a minute," he said, and sprinted off.

"Don't go, Ben!" called Liz.

Kate whimpered. "I don't want Ben to go."

Alfred looked round, as if trapped. "I'll get her! Can't have gone far yet. Ben!" he shouted. "Come back here and look after your own fucking family! I'll sort her out!"

He swung round on one foot and started up the cliff path, skipping from rock to stone.

Liz and Kate stood together, watching.

"Let's go and see if Ben's all right," said Kate tugging at Liz's hand.

"Yes. Okay," Liz decided.

Hand in hand they went up the cliff path.

The path took them past the rock pools where the children had played, then twisted round the headland to the higher ground. They'd often walked that way together, as Liz had done with her father as a child; they knew to keep away from the heather that hid the cliff's edge and the warning roar of the waves.

Light was beginning to fade into grey; pale shadows flickered out of nowhere. Liz held fast to Kate's hand so neither stumbled. She could smell warm gorse and sharp gusts of sea-salt air as they panted onwards. She listened for Ben's voice, but heard only seagulls calling derisively in the distance.

There was no trace of them – no footprints, no swaying bracken where someone might have passed, no faraway figure.

"Come on, Mummy," said Kate, sensing Liz's anxiety.

"Don't worry. We'll catch up with them soon." She speeded up. Surely there should be some sign of them by now? "Ben!" she shouted. "Ben! Answer me!" And Kate's thin voice echoed hers.

They were approaching the highest point of the

headland, where the grey sea seemed to surround them as the ground sloped away in a tangle of rocks and bracken and rough heather.

There were three figures. Liz could see the outline of Megan, back to the sea, wiping her nose on the sleeve of the dirty white coat, hat still jammed on her head. Alfred was ignoring her, leaning, one elbow against a rock.

Ben hadn't seen them arrive; his attention was fixed on Megan. Liz felt Kate tug at her hand and point at him.

Ben was speaking quietly to Megan. "It's all right, Megan," he was saying. "He'll take you home soon. Or if he doesn't, I will – I know the way."

"What are you on about, baby Ben? Leave her to me – I know how to handle her – don't I, Megan?" Alfred, sprang out of his relaxed pose, turned suddenly towards her. She stepped back in alarm.

Liz stopped herself from crying out in warning and frightening Megan further.

"Come on, this way, Megan." Ben was holding out his hand, trying to coax her to away from the cliff's edge.

"Leave her be – let her do what she wants!" said Alfred roughly.

"But she's too near…"

Alfred rushed over to Ben and grabbed him by the shoulders, shaking him violently. "You just leave us alone, little boy! I can do what I like! I'm still stronger than you, even if you did push me downstairs. I can push you, matey, right over this –"

Kate screamed.

Liz ran forward and grabbed Alfred by the hair. "Don't –"

Alfred, stunned for a moment, twisted out of Liz's grasp, punching her hard in the ribs so she fell. Kate rushed over to her mother, and tried to pull her up. "Mum! Mummy!" she wailed.

Liz, clutched her arms round her ribs, struggled to her feet. "I'm OK," she breathed with difficulty. "Get back! Out of the way!" She led Kate towards the path.

Ben looked from his mother to Megan in bewilderment. Then he lurched across the grass, pulled Megan back towards safety, and began flailing his arms wildly towards Alfred.

"Not much of a boxer, are you, baby Ben?" Alfred jeered, dancing round Ben's windmilling figure. "No proper training in your posh school, eh?"

Ben landed a blow on Alfred's arm.

"Fuck you!" Alfred swore. "That was my bad shoulder!"

Ben nearly apologised.

"Don't hurt him," Megan was sobbing again. "Poor Alfred." She sank down onto the grass, holding her hands out to him.

"Poor Alfred, my arse! Look at posh boy! He couldn't hit a fly in pigshit!" He leapt at Ben, hissing and spitting with rage. "You leave my girl alone! She's my business! I didn't ask you to come poking your nose in – "

"But you locked me up!" Ben's voice was muffled by Alfred's arm, which pressed round his neck.

"Yeah, and a fat lot of good it did me! I even –" he punched Ben at every word – "took you home – and you cheated me, you little bastard, when all I wanted was to see your family and stay with you like a proper person…"

To Ben's horror, Alfred was weeping. He flung away from Ben, hiding his face in the crook of his arm.

"See what you done!" Megan shrieked. "You hurt him!"

"Shut up, you silly bitch!" Alfred scrubbed at his face, sounding reassuringly angry. "It's your fault! If you hadn't come trailing after me, clinging on, I could have made friends."

"I'm your friend," Megan insisted. "I'm your friend, and I help you, don't I? You couldn't get on without me, now could you?"

"Course I could get on without you! I was doing fine here till you turned up"

Megan flung her arms round him. "But you need me! I'm a nurse – I'm useful!" She was wailing loudly again.

"Mummy, make her stop!" Kate shouted.

Liz pulled herself away from Kate and strode towards them.

Alfred was still trying to get Megan away. "Stupid cow!" he shook her roughly. "Get off me, you bitch, you fat, stupid… You're hurting my… Let go!"

Megan was clinging round Alfred's neck, repeating "Wouldn't hurt a fly, me… only come to help you…" while Alfred struggled to unlace her arms and slide free.

Which he did. He slid freely over the edge, feet slithering on the heather, followed by Megan still gripping on to his arm.

The splash was indistinguishable from the beating of the waves against the cliff.

Ben rolled onto his front and wriggled forwards to the cliff edge.

"What the hell are you doing?" Liz yelled.

He dragged himself by his elbows. He could hear his mother calling him to stop, and Kate moaning quietly.

He clung to the heather and peered over the edge. He glimpsed dark waves flinging themselves at the rocks below, exploding into white foam, but nothing solid enough to resemble a face, or a hand.

He heaved himself back and waited until his breathing had slowed. Then he stood up and brushed himself down. "Nothing," he said, walking towards his mother and Kate.

Liz sat with an arm round Kate. "I should have stopped them," she said, trembling.

"How?" said Ben.

"I don't know – not let it begin…"

"It's my fault," said Ben. "I shouldn't have let him near the village – I knew he wanted…"

"What?" Liz asked.

"More," Ben muttered.

Kate was shivering. "Can we go home now?"

Liz put her arms round both children, and hugged

them, breathed in the warmth of their salty, sandy hair.

"Come on, then," she said, taking charge again.

After the long walk home, they lit the sitting-room fire, and sat together exhausted in its comforting light, arms round each other.

"What happened to them, Mummy?" Kate said.

Ben sighed loudly. "You were there, too."

"I thought you were going to save Megan…"

"I meant to," said Ben. "I tried to – but Alfred…" Tears ran down Ben's face. Kate caught the tears with her finger before they got to his chin. "Get off!" he sniffed, pushing her away.

"You saw what happened, Kate. What do you think happens if you fall off a cliff into the sea?" Liz said.

"You die…like Nana and Grampa?" Kate said.

"Well… not quite, but… yes…" Liz began.

"It was my fault," interrupted Ben.

"No it wasn't!" said Liz.

"But if I hadn't gone after her…"

"It was nothing to do with you."

"But we ought to tell a policeman," said Kate.

"Tomorrow," said Liz and Ben together.

"Now," said Liz, "I'm going to heat up some soup, and make toast, and then we're going to bed."

"Can I sleep in your bed?" Kate asked.

Liz lay in bed, trying to avoid Kate's restless legs, thinking of all the things she needed to do. Ask Mrs.

Phillips where to report the accident… send children up to Cyril's – see what he's got in… fish, perhaps? If only we hadn't gone… poor Megan…"

She heard Ben mumbling in his sleep, and then fell asleep herself.

20

Next morning Liz got up quietly and went down to find breakfast. She was hungry. She made herself some tea, and a bowl of oats with chopped apple – the days of cereal were long gone, to Kate's great disgust. "I want Crunchy Nut Cornflakes," she would whine when faced with porridge.

"I can't think why," Liz would say," I never used to buy them anyway – too much sugar!"

"Exactly!" Kate would say triumphantly, as if that clinched the argument.

Liz sipped her tea, and listened. No sound of the children: just occasional footsteps and voices from the road, seagulls, and a small breeze ruffling the apple tree. Apples. Mrs. Phillips had said they should get a good harvest this year, and better next, if she had the tree pruned properly. Mrs. Phillips… "Oh, my god! I must ask her what to do about the accident! Police? Coastguards? Are there coastguards any more?" In another life, she'd always known what to do – who to phone, who to ask, which department to apply to, how to get the form for…

Mrs. Phillips had been up for hours, involved in

some elaborate piece of baking with flour and a rolling pin. "Always like to keep ahead," she said to Liz by way of greeting. "Just making some batches of pastry to freeze. Might as well use the electric while we still have it! But you didn't come for a lecture, though?" she added, seeing Liz's worried face. "I think this is going to be a coffee problem," she said, leading the way to the kitchen, and wiping the flour off her hands. "Sit down, then – I'll make some of the real stuff. You could do with it, by the look of you."

While Mrs. Phillips busied herself about the kitchen, and poured coffee, Liz started her tale "… so there was nothing we could do to save them," she ended. Her hands shook round the coffee cup.

"And Kate?" asked Mrs. Phillips.

"Well… shocked. We did talk about it. She was the one who said we must tell a policeman!" Liz took a deep breath. "And Ben says it's his fault and he should have stopped them. I should have, too. I mean, I'm supposed to be the adult here – and look what I let happen!"

"Oh, it's not as if you personally pushed them over…! Kate's got the best idea so far – you must go to the Police. See what happens."

"What do you think might happen?"

"To be honest, I don't think they'll take much notice. Who were these two, after all? Where did they come from? – No, don't tell me – I don't need to know. You'll have to report it, otherwise what'll the children think? We must still try to do the right thing, after all.

Now look, have a nice walk into town, get something delicious for supper, and see what the Police say. And if you find anyone selling lamb chops... I could do with a treat too..."

Liz got up from the table, and hugged Mrs. Phillips for the first time. "I knew you'd make me feel better," she said.

"Works two ways," said Mrs. Phillips gruffly. "Go on with you, now – get those children helping you!"

They walked into town, carrying a bag each. "You never know what we might find," said Liz encouragingly.

"Dead cabbage?" suggested Ben.

"Got that in the garden," said Kate. "What about horrible doggy bones?"

"Horrible bones make delicious soup," said Liz.

"Not likely!" said Ben shuddered.

"We'll just have to see what we find, and do our best," Liz said.

Ben snorted. "Yeah, dead cabbage and bones."

"Or... green sprouty potatoes and fatty bacon!" suggested Kate, screwing up her nose in disgust.

"And caterpillar cabbage with... pigs' arses!" Ben went on.

Liz caught up with Ben and hugged him, happy he seemed to be able to joke about food now.

"What's that about?" he asked, as Kate clamoured for a hug, too.

"Hush! Here's the butcher's," said Liz.

They bought Mrs. Phillips's lamb chops, then mince, sausages, and some stewing lamb.

"All local," said the butcher. He wrapped the purchases in brown paper and tied the parcel with string. "How's the family?" he asked as he took the money.

"Mostly dead," said Kate, before Liz could speak.

"Kate!" Ben kicked her on the ankle.

Liz hustled them out of the shop. "Whatever…?" she began.

Kate was crying. "I only wanted to stop him," she wailed. "You got so sad last time…"

"What's she on about?" asked Ben. "Mum…?"

"Oh, I got upset… before you came back…"

"And Mum cried and Mari helped us," added Kate.

"Right… Okay…" said Ben, perhaps now realising they'd had problems, too. Tonight, perhaps, after supper, he'd ask their story.

They scanned other food shops, and found local cheese, potatoes, some dried apricots and prunes, weighed out into brown paper bags. Liz stocked up.

"But I don't like prunes," Kate whined.

"You will when I make nice pudding out of them – do you remember that, Ben?"

Ben nodded and helped himself to an apricot. "These are good, too," he said.

"I want one!" Kate demanded.

They walked along the High Street chewing, until Liz said, "Enough! We need to keep some for the store-cupboard! And anyway, we're here, now."

The grey stone façade of the Police Station, with its heavy wooden door and blacked-out windows, appeared before them.

"Police. Swyddfa Heddlu," Kate read slowly. "But I don't want to go in there – it's too dark!"

"Well, you said we should go, and I'm not leaving you outside after last time," said Liz.

Last time ? Ben wondered. He obviously had some catching up to do. Not least learning to speak Welsh as well as his sister.

The policeman at the desk put his jacket on as they came in.

"Don't usually get visitors at this time of day! How can I help?" he asked, smiling kindly at Kate.

"We've come to report an accident," Liz said before Kate could blurt out their story.

"Ah," he pulled out his notebook towards him. "Now, someone lost something? Little girl lost her bucket and spade?" He chuckled across the desk at Kate.

"No!" she answered crossly. "They fell over the cliff. Alfred and Megan, I mean – Alfred tried to…"

Liz caught Kate by the arm. "There was a serious accident."

The policeman looked at them. "Come by here." He lifted up a flap in the counter to let them through into a dingy room containing three chairs and a narrow table. "Sit down," he said. He sat on the chair by the desk; Liz and Ben took the other two. Kate leant against her mother.

"Right," he said. "I'm Detective Sergeant Daffydd Jones. "Now, first, I need your names, and addresses."

They went over the events, several times, from the moment Ben had met the victims, to his journey back home – minus the break-in, of course. Sometimes the sergeant asked Liz; sometimes he asked Ben. Now and then he looked at Kate. Sometimes D.S. Jones shook his head; sometimes he scratched his nose; sometimes he sighed. Liz gave her version; Ben gave his. All the time D.S. Jones scribbled on a large lined pad in front of him.

"Did you actually see them in the water, then?"

"No," Ben admitted. "Didn't see them in it. I just assumed…"

"It was getting dark," Liz said.

"And are they telling the truth, young lady?" he appealed to Kate at last. "Is that how it happened?"

Kate had had enough. She nodded, her face white with exhaustion. "Yes," she said. "I told you – they fell over the cliff. Can we go home now, please?"

D.S. Daffydd Jones glanced back over his notes. "We-e-ell," he said. "As long as you don't move house, or leave the country, I reckon you can go. If we hear any news about your friends, we'll let you know."

"They're not our friends," said Ben.

"Manner of speaking," said the policeman. "I'll show you out."

"Well, that wasn't so bad, was it?" said Liz.

"But he's let us go!" said Ben.

"Yes. Did you think he'd lock us up?"

Liz shepherded them into a café.

As Ben and Kate read the brief menu, Liz reassured them – the police were probably far too busy coping with local problems to deal with the accidental death of strangers.

"What local problems?" Ben said, looking up from the choice between beans and sausage or beans and eggs.

"Lorries getting hijacked, food being stockpiled, strangers wandering about – the police have to try to keep things under some sort of control. And that takes time and effort…"

"But they died!" said Ben.

"A lot more people might die if the Police don't keep order! That's what people say, anyway."

The waitress was hovering, so they gave their orders. There was no Coca Cola, but neither Ben nor Kate complained.

"We'll be all right," said Liz, forking up tepid beans.

"Course we will," said Ben.

Kate shrugged. "Can I have some more water, please?"

"'May I'," said Ben, kicking her under the table. "Now say it in Welsh, show-off!"

To his intense irritation, she did.

21

The garden was coming on well, now that both Ned and Ben were working on it. The first bed had been expanded, and two others had been dug. One was waiting for potatoes, and now Liz had a herb bed. The tiny pear tree she'd planted at its centre had already gained height. There was thyme, oregano, rosemary, and mint which was spreading like a weed

"I said to put it in an old bucket," said Ned. "Can't stop mint when it gets a hold."

"I'll dry it and sell it at Cyril's. Or at the market."

"That's what you think," said Ned. "Every bugger's got mint coming out of their ears, now, what with the lamb and the tatws. What you want to do, now, if you want to sell stuff, is grow something a bit special. Different."

"What about chillies?" said Ben.

"I don't have any seeds," Liz began.

"Yeah, you do! Remember when I asked you for matches for the picnic fire? I was looking through the kitchen drawer, I thought I'd found some – but they weren't – they were chilli seeds!" Ben was triumphant.

"Oh!" said Liz. "They came from that Mexican restaurant we used to go to in London. They gave the seeds away, little seeds on sticks… They'll be much too old, surely?"

"Worth a try," said Ben, and he set off to rummage for the seeds and flower pots.

"Can I help?" called Kate, emerging pink and hot from the tent she'd made from the old clothes' horse and a blanket.

"Suppose so," said Ben. "You can plant a seed for every flower pot you find."

That's the way, Liz thought. Little steps at a time. We'll make this life work… Still money coming in, so we'll be all right for a while, as long as he remembers… Not that there's anything to buy now, except food, and a lot of that's bartered, anyway… As long as the children are happy…

Ben and Kate appeared up the garden steps, bickering about the best place to keep the pots of chilli seedlings.

So that's all right, then, Liz thought.

Ben was in the garden before supper. He'd picked a couple of lettuces, some spring onions, and a bunch of herbs – chives and rocket – anything to add a bit of flavour to Kate's sodding lettuce, basically.

They now made the evening meal together. Kate enjoyed helping chop and stir, and Ben devised new ways of cooking the same old things. "We could cut the cabbage really thinly, and cook it in the frying pan, with some garlic, perhaps," he suggested one day.

"Sounds great," said his mother. "Where did you get that idea?"

Ben shrugged. Maybe he'd seen Rufus do it, or even Megan. He still worried about the two from the Chocolate Farm. Suppose they were still looking for him? He always felt uneasy.

His mother was constantly watching him too, measuring his mood. She often said, "We're making a new life together here, and we're doing pretty well – things will be fine."

She was probably right, but he couldn't help thinking it was easier if you were Kate's age, or had been born here, like Mari, or if you were old, like Mrs. Phillips. I can't just sail on as if nothing mattered except the next meal. What's going to happen? What about school? I can't even speak the language… And if those two come back… He found himself squeezing the lettuces till they went floppy.

"Where's that salad?" Liz called. "It'll need washing."

"Coming," he said and went to shake the lettuces vigorously under the running tap, swirling the water round the leaves.

"You don't have to kill them! Oh, and next time, use a bowl of water – it's a waste to let the tap run like that. Suppose the water gets cut off?"

Ben dumped the lettuce into the colander, and

stalked off to the sitting-room. He threw himself on the sofa and picked up his book, but couldn't read. He was still frightened. All the scary moments he'd gone through on the way to Wales clung round him in a kind of fog. He'd coped, and his mother was proud of him, but that period of his life, as she said, was over.

"Now we have to move on, get on with the next job, take the next little step," his mother said. He began to find her homilies intensely irritating.

"Turn that noise down – I'm trying to read!" he shouted towards the kitchen as the radio blared.

"We're lucky we've still got local broadcasting," his mother called back. "It's better than nothing."

"Not when you can't understand a fucking word of it!" Ben muttered, sullenly.

"Then it's time you made a bit of effort to learn some Welsh!" she said, appearing in the doorway, hands on hips. "Look how Kate's doing, and even mine's coming back, what with Mari and the radio. Mari would help you, too, I know…"

"I am making an effort, all the fucking time!" Ben shouted. "I make an effort with the garden, and the dinners, and… and… just being here! And I don't want that woman teaching me Welsh for kiddies!"

"But I can talk grown-up Welsh, can't I, Mum?" said Kate anxiously, peering under her mother's arm.

"Yes, yes, of course – you're beginning to."

"But I can now!" Kate's voice rose.

Ben stomped out of the room and slammed the

front door. He couldn't stand both of them fussing. He thought about going to the beach for some peace, but then he remembered. Can't even enjoy the place like we used to, in case…

He sat on the steps up to the garden. He knew what he had seen: Alfred and Megan had gone over the cliff, and there was no way anyone could survive a fall like that.

But.

Wouldn't the bodies wash ashore? He remembered going to the Ferry with his father, ages ago, and hearing the old fishermen muttering together in Welsh, then talking to his father as though he were a stranger to the village. "You mind where you let the boy swim – treacherous currents in these parts. Lost someone a few weeks back – swam round the rocks then swept away – body ended up round Moylegrove – unrecognisable, it was!"

Ben had cringed as his father blustered, "Oh, we're used to it round here – wife grew up here, you know. Do a bit of sailing, too, so we know about currents…" His dad once tried to sail round the headland, and had to be rescued.

"Over-confidence is as dangerous as ignorance," his mother had yelled. "You can't know the sea after a dozen bloody sailing lessons!"

Ben had been torn between sympathy with his father for being shouted at, and shame at him for being such a complete dick.

It bothered him to think about his father. Bloody typical, he thought, never here when things are really difficult – never stays to help. And we're fine without him. Then he remembered the money that was still coming into their account. They wouldn't have done so well without that. Typical Dad, again, he thought. Just throw money at problems, or turn up with treats. No idea that we might like him to actually be here. He tried to remember when they had all pitched in as a family. It always seemed to be Mum who was left to cope.

He sighed deeply.

A sudden voice made him jump.

"You seem to have the cares of the world on your shoulders. Can anyone help?" It was Mrs. Phillips. "I was just calling to see you mother about shopping for tomorrow."

Oh, god – shopping and food again, Ben thought. "I'm okay," he mumbled.

"But it's not easy, is it?" To Ben's horror, she sat down beside him on the step. "You've done the hardest part, which was getting here – now you've got to sort out how to keep going – that right?"

Ben nodded. She was right, but he wished she'd shut up.

"And then there'll be school – is that a problem?"

"Welsh," said Ben.

"They do teach it in the secondary schools, I believe. And there are always evening classes to start you off."

"Really?" said Ben. "I didn't…"

"You thought you had to be fluent from the start? Well, how many people round here aren't Welsh at all – how do you think that works?"

"Most of the people we know are Welsh, though," Ben said.

"Learn from them, then! And come and practise your English on me when you start to forget it!"

Ben laughed in spite of himself.

"That's better!" Mrs. Phillips said. "It's the least of your worries, really, though, isn't it? I'll tell you what you need," she said, heaving herself up from the step.

Oh, god – here we go again – everyone knows what I need better than I do! Ben thought ."What?" he asked, trying to sound polite.

"A job," she said. "Something to take your mind off things."

Ben nodded. "Yeah, but…" he began.

"You could try the couple down at the Ferry – they always need washing-up done, if nothing else. Tell your mother I'll talk to her in the morning."

Ben waited until he saw her hall light go on, and then let himself back into the house. He slunk off to bed without saying goodnight.

Might be an idea, he thought. Then I could earn some money for us, and we wouldn't be so dependent on Dad's…

He woke late, and listened to the familiar sounds of the house: his mother clattering in the kitchen, Kate running in and out, banging doors and singing, the mewl and scratching of the seagulls on the slate roof. He lay for a while trying not to be awake, then pulled on his clothes.

"Just going out for a bit," he called to his mother.

"Don't you want breakfast?" she asked. "Have you washed? And where are you going?"

"Down the pub!" he replied. "Shan't be long!" and ran out of the house before there were any more questions. He jogged down the road to the Ferry.

He'd been there often enough with his parents. His father had called it their "local" with that proprietary manner of his – "Two pints of Felin Foel and a ginger beer shandy," he'd say," And have one yourself, my old friend." The barmen would exchange knowing looks. Sometimes they had eaten there, and his dad embarrassed him again when he tried to engage the chef in conversations about local food – "Of course, if you had lamb of this quality in London, you could charge an arm and a leg – that's the trouble with the Welsh – no idea of marketing. Now if…" He was oblivious of other people's feelings. Sometimes his mother would interject to turn the conversation.

"Don't see the problem, "his father would say later. "They're English, here, anyway…"

Now as Ben pushed his way through the swing doors, breathing in the familiar smell of beer and frying onions, he prayed the owners would have forgotten him. No such luck.

"What can I do for you, young Ben?" said a large man in checked chef's trousers, who was wiping tables with an old tea towel. Marcus.

"You used to come in with your mum and dad and the baby – come in for a pint, now have you?" And he chuckled until his chins shook.

"No, no, "Ben stammered. "I can't, yet…"

"Joke," said Marcus seriously.

Ben managed a smile. "I wondered if you wanted any help."

"When you say 'help'," Marcus began, "you mean with cleaning, or cooking, or peeling, or washing, or…"

"Stop pissing about, Marcus – ask the boy properly!" Roger appeared from behind the bar. He was small and bearded and as cross-looking as Ben remembered. He scowled. "What do you want – Ben, isn't it?"

"I wondered if you needed any help, cleaning, or washing-up… But I expect you want people with experience… I've done stuff at home, though…"

Roger frowned. "You're not exactly selling yourself, are you? What makes you think we might need help?"

"I – I don't know, really – it's just that Mrs. Phillips said…"

"Ah! Mrs. Phillips!" said Roger. "Why didn't you say so before?"

"The correct answer to that is 'You didn't ask me'," said Marcus.

"Old friend of ours – saved us from a fate worse than closure when the villagers turned holy… I think this calls for chips," said Roger, and he jerked his head at Marcus, who obediently went towards the kitchen. "Now, sit down, and tell me your life story."

By the time Ben had finished giving a truncated account of his journey to the village, Marcus was back with a huge bowl of golden chips. "No shortage of potatoes yet! Tomato ketchup or mayonnaise?" he asked.

"Mayonnaise," said Ben, who had never had chips with mayonnaise before.

"I fancy we might have a bit of a foodie here," said Marcus. "Possible joke."

"Eat!" said Roger.

The chips were probably the best Ben had ever eaten – crisp and salty, and soft in the middle. Mayonnaise went well, he discovered. Still, he poured ketchup on his second helping.

"So," said Roger eventually, when they had all finished eating, "the boy needs a job, and we need a washer-upper. And how do we pay him?"

"Oh, money, please," said Ben anxiously.

"I was thinking chips," said Marcus. "Joke," he added as he saw Ben's face fall.

"I think we can manage a small wage," said Roger, frowning thoughtfully at Ben. "When can you start?"

"Oh – now – when would you like?"

"Perhaps you should let your mum and dad know?" Roger said

"Oh, they won't mind – my dad's not around, anyway – just Mum and Kate, my little sister."

"And they don't matter?" Roger growled.

"Yeah, of course they do – they'll be pleased."

"Right," said Roger. "If they're okay with it, you can start this evening. Five o'clock sharp."

"Wages docked if you're late," said Marcus.

"Joke," said Ben, before Marcus could. "I'll be there."

22

Ben was too busy and tired to worry any more. He washed and dried up – "I will not have smeary glasses," Roger barked – and was proud when Marcus let him chop onions for a stew, or shred cabbage for salad.

"Dab hand," said Marcus. "No joke."

Roger steered him away from the bar saloon – "Too young to drink, too young to serve," he said, but before long Ben found himself helping with most of the pub work. "If anyone asks, you've just popped in for a sarnie. Don't suppose they will – anything goes these days – they don't even think of us as devil's spawn anymore. I quite miss it, really. They'd come in, the old men, drink like fish, then leave spouting some homily on the sanctity of marriage…"

Ben saw that, though Roger could hardly bring himself to speak to anyone, other than by way of a satirical aside, Marcus regularly came out of his kitchen to chat cheerfully with the customers. The tourist trade had stopped, but there was still a steady trade of local drinkers. Gone was the habit eating out: there was neither money nor supplies for elaborate meals, so Marcus's orders were mostly sandwiches, cawl and ploughman's lunches.

"My talents are wasted," he said dramatically. "Home-made bread and local cheese though – your dad would like that." He nodded at Ben. "What happened to him – do you know?" he asked. "Is he dead?"

Ben was startled. "Don't think so," he said. "Went to the city and never came back."

"Joke?" asked Marcus.

"No," said Ben, and he returned to chopping an onion.

Ben was also too preoccupied to worry about school. He enjoyed talking to the customers when he got the chance, and was beginning to understand when they teasingly ordered in Welsh. The first time he tried answering in kind, a cheer went up, and even Roger smiled.

At home he asked Kate to help him learn some useful phrases.

"I don't know words for drinks," she said, "but I know 'what do you want?' and 'please' and 'thank you' and stuff, and I can talk about the weather and things like that."

Ben accepted her help gratefully, and although his latest phrase sometimes triggered a flood of incomprehensible Welsh, he could join in the laughter without embarrassment. Ned was a frequent visitor – "Rye's gone to her sister's," he'd say – and he helped Ben sort out who was winding him up and who was putting in a genuine order.

"Quite the little star!" said Roger. "You'll want a pay rise next!"

"Joke," said Marcus seriously. "He knows the state of the till, by now."

Ben was delighted with his small wage. He hid the cash in his room at the back of a drawer: he didn't want to be tempted into spending. He liked the feeling of having a wodge of cash handy, in case his father's money suddenly ran out.

"They are paying you, those two?" his mum asked one day.

"Yes, of course," he answered. "Wouldn't do it for nothing. And Dad's money's still coming in, isn't it?"

"Yes, yes," said his mother. "As long as you're okay," she said, giving him a hug.

But in a corner of his mind he was still worried. He would face school when it happened, but the accident still haunted him. What had really happened? And his father's absence was the only constant thing about him – what kind of person left his wife and children and never bothered to contact them? Ben knew his father had an important job – he'd never been clear what, exactly. He couldn't talk to his mother – it would be embarrassing, and somehow, unkind. So they rarely spoke about him; he seldom figured in their joint memories.

Unlike Nan and Gramps.

"Nan made this when I was little," his mother would say, stroking the quilt on her bed. Or, "If Gramps was here, he'd mend it in no time," she'd say, as the knob of the kitchen door fell off yet again, and she and Ben tried to mend it.

But there was nothing – except their income – to remind them of Michael. "Who's Michael?" Kate asked once, when his mother mentioned the name. Her mother gave her a strange look.

"He's your father. And Ben's," she said. "You know that really, don't you?"

"I forgot," said Kate. "Don't see him much, anyway."

"He's always working," said Ben. "That's why we've got money in the bank." His mother stared at him. Well, someone ought to stick up for him, thought Ben.

Kate often talked about their grandparents, and still cried for them. "I used to cry for you," she said to Ben. "But you're here now."

"Crying doesn't bring people back," Ben said.

"You came back!" Kate insisted.

"I was coming, anyway," said Ben, "Do you cry for Dad?"

"I used to, a bit," Kate admitted. "He used to take me out and buy me things."

"Me, too," said Ben.

When Ben arrived at the pub some time later, it was strangely quiet, as if someone had just stopped talking about him. "Am I going to be sacked?" he wondered. "Maybe they can't afford to pay me any more – or maybe I'm useless and they're sick of me."

Ben busied himself until the lunchtime trickle began,

polishing glasses and chopping salad for sandwiches. Then he went to the bar to wipe the tables.

"Hey!" said Roger

Ben turned to look at him. His expression was almost sympathetic.

"What?" Ben frowned.

"You know that accident?"

"Yeah," said Ben. He dropped the cloth and leant against the table, feeling suddenly wobbly.

"They've found them. The bodies, that is. Police came asking for you this morning. Well, 'police'. Detective Sergeant Jones. No idea how he knew you were here. Thought he was coming to arrest me for employing a minor. He was asking for you. Better nip off home now and see what's happening."

"Hope it's the news you want!" called Marcus from the kitchen.

Ben didn't answer. He hardly knew what he hoped to hear.

"Mum!" he shouted as he came in.

"In here," she replied, from the sitting room where she sat drinking tea with D.S. Jones.

The policeman greeted Ben like an old friend. "How's it going?" he asked. "Hear you're busy down the road?"

Ben nodded, and waited.

"Well. Straight to the point. We've found a couple of bodies, up the coast a bit." D.S. Jones scratched his nose "If your ma gives the go-ahead I'd like you to come with me to the cottage hospital to identify them. Only place we can keep bodies nowadays, Mrs. Patterson," he explained, turning to Liz.

"Is that all right, Ben?" she asked, looking at him anxiously. "I have to come, too, because you're a minor. Kate will stay with Mrs. Phillips, so…"

"It's all right," said Ben. "I bet I've seen more dead bodies than he has!" He turned to the policeman.

"Yes, well," he said. "Not a competition, bach – just a matter of identifying your friends."

"They're not my friends!"

"Maybe so," said D.S. Jones. "But if you and your ma wouldn't mind coming with me in the police car, we can get to town and get the job over."

Police car! thought Ben. Brilliant! Everyone will know, now!

The car park at the cottage hospital was almost empty.

"No one here?" asked Ben in surprise.

"Come here to die, mainly. They're real quick at pulling the Carriers out of the mainstream. Not that there's so many of them, now, so something must be working."

The hospital smelt of floor polish and disinfectant. There was no one to meet them. D.S. Jones led them along several dismal corridors with posters exhorting you to "Eat a balanced diet!" and to "Wash infection away!" Then, gripping cold iron handrails, they went down flights of stone staircases until they reached the basement.

"I'll check it's okay to go in." D.S. Jones tapped at a door with panes of bubbly glass and disappeared.

"All right?" His mother put her hand on his shoulder. Ben nodded.

They were beckoned inside a large room lit by old fluorescent tubes, shiny trolleys down one side and wide stainless steel sinks on the other. In front of them was a wall of lockers. A thin man in a white coat pulled one open as they entered.

"Lab. Technician," said D.S. Jones quietly. "Now if you don't mind…?

The technician slid the drawer out to reveal a white-sheeted body. He parted the covering over the face.

"Is that her?"

Ben looked quickly. "Yes," he breathed.

Megan's face was white and bruised; there was a large gouge on the side of her head. She looked odd without her white hat. He hadn't liked her, but she had fed him.

"That's Megan," said Ben, shuddering.

"Megan what?" asked the policeman.

"Never knew," Ben replied.

D.S. Jones cleared his throat. "And the next," he said.

The technician pulled open another drawer. It's routine to him, Ben thought, and remembered how he'd got used to burying the bodies at the farm. They were bodies though – he hadn't met them."

He looked at the face. It was wrinkled, whether from seawater or age was hard to tell; the hair was dark, and curly, the nose was narrow and hooked.

"No," said Ben.

"What do you mean, 'no'?" asked D.S. Jones.

"I don't know him. It's not Alfred," said Ben.

"You sure, now?"

"Course I'm sure! I worked with him – travelled with him! It's not Alfred!"

He felt his mother's restraining hand on his arm. He shook it off. "But it isn't, mum, is it? You saw him – you talked to him!"

"Perhaps the sea…?" said his mother hesitantly.

She hadn't been standing as close he had. He pushed her nearer so she had a clearer view.

"You're right," she said. "This one's too old." She sighed and slid to the floor.

In the fuss that followed, Ben heard D.S. Jones calling for people, arranging tea, somewhere to recover, and, most of all, apologising.

They sat in a small visitors' room that looked out over the car park.

"Sorry, Mrs. Patterson. So sorry about that. Just me wanting it all cleared up and tidied away, see?"

"It's all right. Surprise, that's all," she said, clinging on to Ben's hand, which, for once, he didn't snatch away.

Later, when he'd driven them home, D.S. Jones apologised again, and they served him more tea.

"My fault, really, mum," said Ben. "Shouldn't have made you go so near."

"Surprised you could stomach it," said the policeman, looking hard at Ben.

Ben scuffed the mat with his foot. "Used to it," he said at last. "That's how I met Alfred…"

"The Chocolate Factory?"

Ben looked up.

"Oh, we know about places. Little we can do about it, though – even if we wanted to. There's some who'd argue that they do a useful job – keeping the Carriers away from towns – looking after them…"

"Suppose so," Ben began. "But it's illegal, isn't it? I mean, families ought to be told. People shouldn't be left to guess."

"There's legal and legal," said D.S. Jones heavily. "Mostly if the Carriers are Runners, too, it's because they haven't got a family worth speaking of. And at least they've got somewhere to be, for a while…"

"How do you know all this?"

"What do you think the 'D' in 'D.S.' stands for, then? Detective – got exams to prove it!" D.S. Jones chuckled. "Word gets around, in my line of business. Lorries still come through – drivers like a chance for a bit of a drink and a chat – and then people visit their da-in-law's sister's niece… surprising what you can pick up!" He stood up to leave. "Now, if you do hear anything or see anything of that other young man – I'm not saying you will – he might well be the bottom of the sea, but if – you just let me know, right?"

"I was sure it would be him," said Ben after he'd driven away.

"Me too," said his mother.

"I really wanted him to be dead, so that it was all finished and tidy, like D.S. Jones said... I don't want to feel he's out there still looking for me."

"He can't do anything, though – it's all out in the open. People know where you belong; the police know where he comes from... You're not in danger."

"I know – but I still feel I might bump into him at any moment."

"Doesn't necessarily mean that he's still around," said his mother slowly. "Remember what D.S. Jones said?"

"Yeah, yeah! I wish he was at the bottom of the sea – it would be so much easier!"

The back door banged, and Kate came bounding back from Mrs. Phillips's house.

"What would be easier?" she asked. "Me and Mrs. Phillips have just finished our story, and we're going to do another one and this time it's going to have pictures and I'm going to do them because she says I draw better than she does, so I said she ought to write the story then, because she... What?"

"Wonderful!" said her mother. "Can't wait to read it!"

"Oh, me too," said Ben, as his mother nudged him.

"So are they dead?" Kate asked.

"Well, they haven't found Alfred yet," Liz admitted reluctantly, watching Kate closely.

"That's good, then, isn't it? It's not nice to be dead."

"But at least you know where people are!" Ben burst out. "Not lurking about waiting to catch you!"

"Ben," said his mother. "Don't frighten her!"

"I'm not frightened." Kate tossed her head, and went out to play in the garden.

"I'm not frightened, either," said Ben. "I'm just not – comfortable! Right – I'm going back to work," he said, slamming out of the house before his mother had time to say anything else.

Liz wasn't feeling comfortable, either. Uncertainty seemed to cling round Alfred. He's only a boy, she told herself. He probably just wants to be friends – misses his family. Then she realised she was still thinking about him in the present tense, and remembered how she'd felt on the beach. Silly to feel at risk from someone who wasn't even there.

Ben pounded down the road to the pub. He was glad to be able to spend time away from his family. Roger and Marcus were friendly, but detached, unlike his mother and Kate whose solicitude was suffocating.

He shoved open the pub door and stamped in.

"The wanderer returns," said Roger.

"Sorry," said Ben.

"So was it Alfred, then?" said Marcus, popping his head out of the kitchen.

Ben shook his head.

"Well, while you're here, you might as well start washing up," said Roger. "We don't have time to ponce about listening to gossip. Hop to it! – Don't worry," he said quietly, as Ben passed him. "Things are never as bad as they seem."

"No, they're sometimes worse," Ben said, and felt, rather than saw, the look Roger and Marcus exchanged.

23

The first day of school was fast approaching. Kate was spending a lot of time with Mari, practising her Welsh. She tried it out on Ned when he came to dig in the garden, but he refused to play.

"Need to be born to it," he said churlishly. "We can all talk the English, down here. No need for you to bother."

"Don't put her off!" Auntie Rye said, when she heard. "She's making an effort, which is more than some!"

Ned gave his coughing laugh. "I remember the father – 'Borrow dah,' he'd say, as if he was giving me a present!"

"Yes, well…" said Auntie Rye. "But our Liz, now – she was born to it, and it's coming back to her now. And her boy – he's learning fast, from what I hear in the pub."

"Wouldn't know," said Ned. "Don't know what goes on down there."

"Is that so?" said Auntie Rye, sniffing meaningfully.

"I need new clothes for school," Kate announced at breakfast one morning.

"You're right. We'd better find out what you need," said her mother.

Liz had enrolled Kate at the school, but no one had said anything about uniform. She asked Mari that afternoon.

"No, no," she said. "They don't do that – people can't afford it."

"At my old school we had tunics and shirts and indoor shoes and gym shoes… and a blazer and a hat and…" wailed Kate.

"All that for one little girl!" Mari said.

"But can't I wear it anyway, Mum?" Kate pleaded.

Mari shook her head. "Other kids won't be wearing all that," she said gently. "You don't want to look daft, do you?"

"But I didn't look daft, did I, Mummy?"

"No, because all the others were wearing the same things, love. That's what uniform means. It's a different uniform here. You can still have some new clothes – you're growing out of your jeans, anyway…"

"Can I wear those to school?"

Liz looked at Mari for help who said, "Why not?"

"Right!" said Kate. "I'll go and make a list – new jeans and sweatshirts and t-shirts and – trainers?"

"If we can find them," said her mother.

Kate swept off to write her list.

"Thanks, Mari," said Liz.

"Well, she's made her own uniform now," said Mari. "Jeans and t-shirts – that's what they all wear these days."

"We'll have to get you kitted out, too, Ben," his mother said.

"They don't wear uniforms at my school, either," said Ben. "I met this kid down the pub who's at my new school, and he said you could wear what you like. So, jeans and t-shirts."

"You'll need new things, though - most of your stuff is too small, and your t-shirts are falling apart…"

"Okay, okay. I'll get some new stuff. With my money. Can I get a lift into town…?"

"You can walk!"

Ben thought he'd done enough walking, but it was fine if she didn't come along: his money, his choices.

Next day, he arrived at the pub and asked for the day off.

Roger wasn't happy. "It's normal to book time off in advance, you know, in an organised world."

"Which it isn't," said Marcus. "So what are you up to, then?"

"That's his business," Roger said. "He can do what he likes on his day off."

"So it's okay?" Ben wasn't sure if a decision had been made.

"Yes, yes – bugger off and leave us with all the work – we'll manage."

Marcus raised his eyebrows at Ben.

"I just want to go shopping," Ben confessed. "I need new stuff for school."

"Christ, I'd forgotten about school," said Marcus.

"Oh, well – that's it, now – the business will go to pot! Joke – almost!" he added.

"I could still work weekends." Ben didn't want to desert his friends.

Roger glared. "Don't be stupid! Normal routine's what you need. Education. Whatever happens, you'll need a good job."

He went on speaking, as Ben tuned out – he sounded like his father, saying stuff about Jobs and The Future. He remembered his mum would say, "Oh, for god's sake, Michael – he's only eight!" and his dad would get angry. Most of their conversations were like that.

"So go on – off to your fashion and fripperies!" Roger was saying.

"Don't buy anything I wouldn't wear," said Marcus.

"Fat chance!" said Ben. "Joke!"

He strolled through the village, waving at Auntie Rye, who was tidying her front garden. "Off gallivanting?" she called, and Ben nodded, laughing.

He passed Cyril leaning in the door frame of his shop as usual. "Leaving already? Village life not good enough, eh?"

"Good morning," he answered, trying to smile.

Mari was coming out of the hairdresser's, with her hair in stiff new waves. "Better now," she said, patting her hairdo. "You going to get yours done for school? You could do with a bit off the length or you'll be plaiting it next!"

Soon he was wandering along hedgerows on the road to town, his first walk alone for a long time.

Automatically he started to scan for food – now there were blackberries coming, and rosehips, and small milky hazelnuts were beginning to appear – then reminded himself that he didn't need to forage. He patted the cash in his pocket as went. Perhaps he'd treat himself to lunch when he'd shopped, in one of those burger and chips or fried chicken places his mother couldn't stand. "You don't know what's in it," she'd say. But Ben didn't care. The pale sunlight was warm on his face and he felt happy.

He'd planned his trip: he'd look round each shop, then go back to buy anything he liked and could afford. He had very little idea of prices – that had been his mother's area, and his father had always sneered that she was too "careful".

The supermarket proved useless – only a few baby and toddler clothes, and not even much food, though the alcohol shelves were full.

He trawled the High Street. Several clothes shops had closed down; there weren't even any charity shops. Then he remembered the market, and found two pairs of jeans on a second-hand stall. The stall-holder let him try them on behind a curtain at the back of her pitch.

"You look nice in them," she said. Ben blushed. "Belonged to my nephew – they come from a nice clean home."

Ben's next success was in an old-fashioned gentlemen's outfitters; "Evans" was written in curvy gold glass script above the door. The window was not enticing – suits, cloth caps and paisley scarves. As he turned to go, the shopkeeper spotted him and beckoned to him over the half-curtain at the back of the window. A bell jingled loudly as Ben pushed the door. The air inside was stale as if no one had ventured inside for years.

"Now," said the man from behind his counter. "I know what you're thinking."

"Well…" Ben began.

"Yes – you're thinking that nothing would induce you to buy anything in this old place. Yes! But I do know what young people want."

Ben nodded, not at all sure that even he knew what young people wanted and wondered how to retreat without causing offence.

The man sprang out and began pulling open glass-fronted drawers. "Look," he said, "You don't want shirts, or waistcoats, or ties." He held up examples of the offending items. Ben shook his head.

"No," said Ben, "All I really need…"

"T-shirts!" said the man, brandishing a plain white t-shirt. "And again!" he produced a black one, then two navy blue ones with long sleeves. "Perfect!" he said. "Aren't they? What you were looking for, am I right?"

"Yes, absolutely," said Ben. "But I…"

"How much? Well… they're on sale – had them for years and can't get rid of them!"

"Why?" Ben began. The t-shirts looked perfectly good to him.

"Pictures!" said the man. "Writing! That's what they all want. I keep up! You have to. As soon as I saw you, I knew – sensible, I thought – wants them for school – am I right?"

Ben nodded and fumbled for his wallet. He wondered if he minded being thought "sensible" and decided that he didn't. He paid, and thanked Mr. Evans.

Lunchtime.

Ben searched up and down the High Street for a greasy spoon. There was the tea-shop place where he'd gone with his mother and Kate after the Police Station, but he didn't want eggs and beans again. Most of the cafés he remembered from childhood trips had gone. He was about to give up and head for home when he remembered pubs. His served food – why not these? Ben found a small stone building at the end of an alleyway which served not only Felin Foel but hamburgers and chips.

The room was low-ceilinged, with small mullioned windows that let in a dim underwater light. A few figures sat drinking in dark corners. He walked up to the bar.

"Don't serve kids," said the barman.

"Can I eat?" said Ben.

"Or English," said the barman.

Ben tried to order in Welsh: burger with chips and onion rings, and water.

"Not bad," said the barman. "Coming up!"

Ben wondered for a moment whether he should walk out, but the frying food smelt good. His money, his day out, his treat to himself.

The burger was sandwiched between two slices of thick crusty bread.

"We don't have buns," said the barman. "But that's real homemade bread, and real beef, too," he added.

"Diolch yn fawr," said Ben politely, and tucked in. It was one of the best burgers he'd ever eaten – and the chips were almost as good as Marcus's. He'd have to bring his mum and Kate, when he'd saved up some more.

He finished and the barman came over to clear his plate.

"Okay?" he asked.

"Bendigedig!" said Ben. It was one of the first words he'd learnt from Kate.

"Enough of that!" said the barman. "You're not Welsh and I don't speak it!"

Ben laughed. "I was coming to the end of my vocab, anyway," he admitted. "Can I have the bill?"

"All done!" The barman tilted his head and glanced over his shoulder towards a dark corner to indicate the presence of an unknown benefactor.

Ben looked round. Someone had risen from a shadowy corner and was walking towards him.

Ben knew that shape, he knew that walk – how was that possible?

The figure leant on his table.

"You enjoy that, then?" Alfred asked.

Ben's mouth hung open.

"Some might say 'Thanks very much'."

Ben tried to speak. He tried to stand up, but his legs didn't work, so he stayed, imprisoned behind his table, back to the wall.

Alfred gazed at Ben, something between triumph and longing in his eyes.

"'Course, I'm a ghost to you," he said, and laughed. "You didn't think you'd get rid of me that easy? I can swim – champion of my school, I was," and he did the familiar little foot shuffle.

"What are you doing here? Where've you been?" Ben said at last. "The police are looking… and Megan…"

"Oh, yes, poor sod," said Alfred. "Sank like a stone."

"I know," Ben said. "I saw her body."

"Go on," said Alfred, with great interest. "How did she look, then?" He sniggered. "What you up to now, then?" He leant in closer.

Ben recoiled. "School," he muttered. "Soon, anyway." He didn't want to tell him anything about his family or his job. "And you?" He couldn't believe that he was making polite chat. He prayed that Alfred was busy doing something, far away, in England, perhaps. "No more farm?" he asked.

"Gave that up. Not the same without mad Megan. Say what you like about her, she knew how to organise."

Ben didn't want to say anything about her; he couldn't banish the picture of her poor bruised face in the mortuary.

"No," Alfred went on, "I'm just marking time for a while. Working here and there. Here, actually – just like you – a washer-upper!"

"How?" Ben stammered.

"Word gets about," said Alfred, tapping his nose.

He was fidgeting, scuffing his feet and pointing over his shoulder. "I reckon I've done you a real good turn again. Not only did I bring you home to little mumsy-wumsy – for which I got no thanks as I remember – but I can now re-unite you with the one that got away – ta da!" he said, waving his arm towards the back of the room.

A figure Ben had known forever came towards him.

Ben sprang up from behind the table, pushing Alfred out of the way.

"Ben," said a familiar voice. "You've grown!"

"Dad?" said Ben. He waited to be hugged; the moment passed. Michael rested his hands on Ben's shoulders.

"How's your mother? And Kate?" he said.

Ben shrugged the hands off. "Where have you been?"

"Oh, it's a long story."

"Why weren't you here with us?" Ben said, feeling anger build.

"Let's sit down and catch up," said his father. Ben let himself be guided back to the table by a hand on his arm.

"Alfred, bring us a pot of tea, and maybe some biscuits if you've got any, there's a good chap," said his father, with a familiarity of tone that bewildered Ben. How did these two know each other?

Alfred disappeared.

"How do you…?" Ben began.

"Met him here, couple of days back, when I drove down to find you all," his father said. "Seems a bright chap – too good for this sort of work. Thought I could give him a bit of a helping hand."

Leaving us to shift for ourselves, Ben thought. He scowled.

"He was the one who put me on to you. Told me his life story, and something in his description of his best helper at the farm struck me… and here we are!" he ended, as if that explained everything.

Ben might have started on his story of Alfred. Instead he said, "You can't have known I'd come in today."

"Of course not!" said his father. "Alfred was going to tell your mother where I was staying, then we'd take it from there. And then you walked in!"

"What are you doing here, though?" Ben persisted. "Why didn't you tell us where you were?"

"You've been all right, though, haven't you?" his father said. "I mean, you all got here safely, and the money's still coming in, right?"

"Depends what you mean by safely," Ben growled.

"Well, you're all here now, and no harm done," his father said." At least you've got a roof – "

Ben couldn't let that go. "Yes, that's mum's, now. Nan and Gramps died."

"Sorry to hear that. But the sickness always gets the old ones first. Shame." He shook his head, then looked Ben in the eye. "I didn't have a very good time, either."

"You were in the City," Ben said.

"Yes, but it wasn't exactly great. People were dropping like flies – the number of guys who got sudden promotions that didn't live to learn the work…!"

"You?" asked Ben.

"I'm here!" his father said. "No, they sent me up to the north of Scotland. We joined a small specialist unit who could run the finances as things got worse. Pretty important work, actually."

"And did they?" Ben spotted Alfred returning and he wanted to end the discussion before he arrived. "Did things get worse?"

"You mean why have they let me go?"

Ben nodded.

"Well, I don't want to raise any hopes, but according to our information, the death rate seems to be stable. The infastructure's taken a bashing, but with proper leadership, I expect we'll all pull through."

"But you didn't know we were all right," Ben insisted.

His father shifted on his chair. "I had a fair idea! You can't do what you like when you're working for the Government, you know. You weren't short of money, after all, and your mother's very capable – you, too, it seems." He patted Ben's arm, awkwardly. "Ah, thanks, Alfred – good lad!" He took the mugs and passed them round. "No biscuits, then?"

Alfred shook his head. "Thought you might like a bit of privacy," he mumbled, turning to leave.

"No, no," said Ben's father. "Sit down and drink up, and we can all go home."

"What? It's not Alfred's home, is it, Alfred? He's not coming with us! Why are you still skulking round here?" Ben asked furiously. "Trying to worm your way into my family again? He can't come with us," he said, turning to his father. "Mum hates him, and he needs to sort things out with the police about Megan, and…"

"I'll be off, then." Alfred stood up to go.

"Hang on, hang on," said Ben's father blustered, getting red in the face. "If I say he can come home, then home he comes."

"Mum's home," said Ben.

"What have the police got to do with anything?"

"Go on, then," Ben prompted Alfred.

"I didn't know they were looking for me, did I? How was I to know? It was nothing to do with me – I didn't know she couldn't swim – it was an accident!"

"Ben?" said his father.

"There was an accident. A girl died. But there's more…" He stopped. He wanted his father to know everything that had happened, but needed to get him alone.

"Ah. Right," said his father. "Well, then, we need to let the police know where he is and sort things out. Alfred? Ben? In fact, right now – we'll go to the Police Station before we drive home. Saves us coming back to town."

Ben stared at his father, astonished. Wasn't it clear that Alfred wasn't welcome? Whose home was it, anyway?

His father got up to leave, pushing Alfred in front of him. "Won't take us long, then you can make a new start. Coming, Ben?"

Ben said nothing. He got up as if to follow them, and as they left the pub, Michael's arm matily across Alfred's shoulder, Ben went into the gents' and waited. No one came to find him. After a while, Ben peered round the door of the pub, glimpsing Alfred and his dad going up the steps of the Police Station. He grabbed his shopping and ran in the opposite direction.

24

"Mum!" Ben shouted, banging the front door behind him and throwing his bags on the floor. "Are they here yet?"

"Who? said his mother, appearing round the sitting-room door. "Kate's gone up to Mari's – she asked Kate if she'd like to help mind Lowri's baby… What's the matter?"

"They've come back," he panted. "Both at once!"

"Slow down."

"It's Dad," he said, trying to stop his voice from squeaking. "I met him in a pub in town. And Alfred was with him."

"You're making it up! Tell me properly." She gripped Ben's hand.

Ben explained.

"But it's not Alfred's home," Liz said.

"I told him!" Ben insisted.

"But what about your dad?"

"Kate will be glad to see him," Ben said.

"And you?"

"I don't know. Will he fit?"

"I don't know, either," said his mother, releasing her hold on Ben's hand, and giving him a brief hug. "We'll have to see. Let's make some supper for the returned wanderer."

"When in doubt, cook," Ben said. "Hey! You're not cooking for Alfred, are you?" he asked, as they began peeling potatoes.

"Chop some onions, and those rashers of bacon, will you, Ben? "Liz began to make cheese sauce.

"Mum!"

"Oh, dear," Liz paused. "Look, let's just see how it goes."

They worked together silence for a while.

"Dad seems dead keen on him – I didn't get a chance to explain – it's so difficult… He's just so plausible!"

A car door slammed and there was a brisk knocking at the front door.

"Oh god!" Liz said, grabbing a tea towel for her wet hands. The knocking came again, louder.

"Liz! Are you there?"

Liz opened the door. Ben peered over her shoulder. "Alfred?" he asked.

"No – the police wanted a talk with him. Aren't you going to let me in?"

Liz and Ben backed out of the way as Michael strode into the narrow hall, Liz hovering by the kitchen door, twisted the tea towel round and round in her fingers. "Hi," she said.

Michael walked towards her, holding out his hands,

but Liz turned away. "Ben," she said, "Nip up the road for me, and get Kate home for supper, will you?"

Don't hurry back, Ben understood, relieved to be out of the way.

"I'd forgotten how small this house was," Michael said. "How ever did we all manage on holiday here?"

He leant against the kitchen wall. He seemed to fill the room.

"It's not a holiday now," said Liz. "Come on. I'll light the fire in the sitting-room."

Michael spread himself over the sofa. Liz put a light to the fire and sat in her mother's little armchair opposite him. He looked much the same: slightly thinner, perhaps, and hair a little greyer, but there were the same restless eyes, the same heavy hands that were never still.

"Quite like old times!" said Michael. "Fire, and all the old things about…"

"So where have you been?" she asked.

"I was just telling Ben, I was sent up to Scotland – only got down here yesterday."

"Scotland's not off the map," said Liz. "You could still phone – to begin with, anyway. Or write? Did you get my letter?"

"That's how I knew where you all were, so I didn't worry – "

"I know you didn't. Not enough to ask how the children were, how I was, how we were coping…"

"You had money!"

"Yes, and a home. But I didn't know where you were or whether you were alive or dead. Imagine how the children felt! You could have died, or been killed by Runners, or arrested by the Cleaners. We had no idea!"

"Doesn't seem to have bothered you that much! You could at least pretend to be glad to see me – I have supported you all this time, after all!"

"I know. Thank you," she said at last. "But I had plans in case…"

"You don't need plans," Michael said, brusquely. "I've still got a job. We'll go back to London together, and start again. Ben can go back to his old school, and Kate can board somewhere as soon as she's old enough."

"Kate's already at school here, and Ben is about to start at the secondary."

Michael sprang up from the sofa and paced the room. "Nonsense, Liz – you can't ruin their lives! We've got to get back to normal."

"This is normal!" Liz shouted. "We've made a new life here!" As Michael started to bluster, she told him quietly all that had happened to them since she'd last seen him, everything. "It's not about money, Michael. Not any more. Haven't you noticed how people are bartering skills and food?"

"Frankly, no!" said Michael. "For god's sake, what skills have you got that would be needed in a place like this?"

Liz knew there was no reasoning with that jeering tone of voice. He'd breezed in and told her what to do, and sneered at how they lived. He wouldn't understand that when Mrs. Phillips gave her vegetables, she'd wash Mrs. Phillips's curtains for her; when she baby-sat for Mari's grand-daughter, Mari would talk Welsh with Liz and Kate, and when Ned did gardening for her, he got to sit in the shed with a couple of bottles of Felin Foel.

She held her shaking hands out to the fire. "This is our home," she said without looking at him.

"Where does that leave me?" he asked.

"It doesn't leave you anywhere – you're free to live where you like, as you always have been."

"But you don't want me living here."

"You wouldn't be happy. You'd always be wanting to do improvements – straighten the walls, put new windows in, pave the garden…"

"It's always worth improving a property – I could help you!"

"It's not a property – it's our home!"

The back door slammed. "Daddy!" Kate called out, as she rushed into the sitting-room and threw her arms round her father's waist. Ben leant against the doorpost.

"My little girl," said Michael, hugging her. "That was something like a welcome!"

"It helps to be young," Liz murmured, as Kate gushed news and questions.

"… but we didn't know where you were," she ended at last.

He shrugged.

"But where were you?" she insisted. "Why didn't you

tell us? Are you going to stay with us now?"

"That depends on your mother," he said, looking at her over Kate's head.

"No!" said Liz. "It depends on all of us. What do you think should happen?" She appealed to the children. "We can go back to London with your Dad, back to your old schools – "

"But are things working in London?" Ben asked. "I mean, we don't know if our schools are still there, or the house – why would it be better there?"

"It's bound to be better in London," said Michael. "There are more schools and hospitals and there's transport and police and things – everything will be back to normal in no time."

"Are there enough people left to run things?" Ben went on. "And how do we know that the disease is really dying out?"

"You have to take a risk now and then! When I was in Scotland – "

"I think I've had enough risks," said Ben quietly.

"I don't want to go back to London," said Kate, from the arm of her mother's chair. She was picking at a loose thread in her jumper. "Why can't we all stay here?"

"We can, of course, if that's what everyone wants," Liz said, holding Kate's hands still.

Michael moved towards the door. Ben got out of his way and went to sit on the floor at his mother's feet.

"You've worked on them well," said Michael without expression. "I did think – but no, never mind. I'll be off, then," Michael said, and he went into the hall, jingling the car keys.

Liz followed him. "What?"

"Well, if you don't know…"

"I wouldn't ask if I knew! But that's always been the trouble!" Liz was having difficulty keeping the tears out of her voice. "You can't be bothered to have a real conversation with me – I always have to agree! And I've cooked supper for us all – I thought you'd like to eat with us."

"I'm not hungry!" he snapped. He went out, slamming the front door. They heard the car drive away.

Liz went back to the sitting-room. The children hadn't moved. "I'm sorry," she said. "I thought at least he'd eat with us."

"Why haven't we got any petrol?" Kate asked.

"Not important enough," said Ben.

Liz returned to the kitchen. The dinner no longer smelled appetising. Had she been fair to Michael when she'd asked the children what they wanted? She'd put them in an impossible position, making them take sides. Yet even Kate wanted to stay in Wales. And Michael had always thought he knew best; he was used to taking important decisions – that was his nature, and the nature of his job. She realised she had never stood against him before.

"Come on," she called. "Let's us eat, anyway, before it burns."

"Not hungry," said Kate.

"Oh, don't you start," said Liz, almost laughing.

"Nice," said Kate as they followed Liz to the kitchen. Liz had laid the table for the four of them, spreading one of her mother's old blue and white linen tablecloths, and putting an earthenware jug of wild flowers at the centre. She'd put out the linen napkins, too, with tumblers and wine glasses. An open bottle of something red stood ready on the draining board.

"Lovely, Mum," said Ben.

"Have to make an effort, sometimes," said Liz, turning to find the casserole, hiding her tears.

None of them did the meal justice. They talked about school, and what they'd take for lunch, and whose alarm clock was most reliable, anything but the subject that seemed to have been decided almost without discussion.

They cleared the table together. Kate shook the cloth outside, Ben put the leftovers in the fridge, and Liz started washing-up.

"What do you really think, you two?" she asked, without looking round at them. "I mean – it's difficult, I know."

There was silence for a moment. Kate had wrapped the tablecloth round her like a cloak, and suddenly Liz was enveloped. She felt Ben patting her shoulder.

"We're okay," he said. "We don't mind."

"You won't miss him?" Tears dripped down Liz's face into the washing-up water.

"I think I missed him in London," Kate said, "but only a bit."

"Oh, Kate!" said Liz, turning round to them. She suddenly felt sorry for Michael. "Why not?"

"He wasn't there much – and I was always in bed. And he's never lived here, except on holidays. And it isn't holiday-time now."

Liz nodded, but she felt guilty at how easily they were writing their father out of their lives. "Of course, he may come back, anyway," she added, trying to sound positive. "When he's had time to think a bit more... he must have been very busy."

Silence.

"Ben...?"

"He's got nothing to do here, has he? There's no jobs in finance, or whatever he does. And we've got school, and stuff... We're used to it."

Later, in bed, she tried not to feel guilty. Kate was looking forward to making friends at school. Ben? He was a serious boy; there had always been a certain reserved air about him, though with school, and now this job at the pub, he seemed to be relaxing a bit. I expect he'll miss the pub when he's at school... she thought. Perhaps I could give them a hand, instead... They'll miss his help... Hope he'll settle at school. If the children were all right, so was she. And the last question that drifted through her head before she fell asleep – the very one she'd been trying to forget – whatever had happened to Alfred...?

25

By half-term, Kate seemed to be coping well with her new school life, but despite Liz's hopes, Ben was becoming more taciturn, limiting his conversation to "What's for supper?" before stomping upstairs to get on with his homework.

"Good day?" Liz always asked.

"All right," he'd mumble from the top of the stairs.

Kate was as vocal as ever. There were endless reports of what Sian had said to Freya, and then what the teacher had said… and then "So it was all right in the end!"

"Well, well," Liz murmured. Sometimes that was enough; Kate would demand food and stories. Sometimes it wasn't – "You never listen to me!" Liz had to calm her ruffled feelings before she, too, stomped off.

There had been no word from Michael, not even to ask about the children. He had never, she reflected, liked situations he couldn't control.

She approached Roger and Marcus at the pub, and promptly found herself employed for the weekday lunchtime service.

"Any experience?" Roger had asked.

"No," she'd confessed, expecting to be shown the door.

"Just like your boy!" he'd said with exasperation. "You run a home – cook – clean, I've no doubt. And what did you do, before all this? Teaching? Well, you can organise, and talk to people."

"You won't make a lot," said Marcus, "but it'll keep you on the straight and narrow. Unlike us! Straight?" He raised his eyebrows dramatically. "Narrow?" and he patted his widening girth. "Joke," he explained. "You'll get used to it."

She enjoyed the work: it was like running a home with grown-ups. She liked talking to the customers, too. When her neighbours found out, they would often call in for a lunchtime sandwich or drink and a chat. Mrs. Phillips would have a dry sherry and egg mayonnaise on wholemeal. "Delicious, Marcus," she would say. "And I didn't have to lift a finger!" Mari, often with the baby in tow, would order a bowl of chips and a Guinness. "Good for my blood pressure." Ned would appear whenever Auntie Rye went to see her sister. "Got a lift with Cyril," he'd say, eyes twinkling. "You can get the petrol if you're delivering. Not a word, now!" Liz would bring him a Felin Foel and a cheese and pickle sandwich. "Proper white bread, I want, mind you."

"Bang goes our chance of getting in *The Good Food Guide*," said Marcus.

"Don't blame Liz – at least she's old enough to bring in some customers," Roger said. "And what's he up to, that boy of yours?"

Liz laughed. "Whatever it is, he's not telling me!"

"Getting on all right with the school work?"

"As far as I know," Liz said. "Teachers have been quite complimentary so far."

"I told him he had to keep at it, not to waste his time hanging around pubs, for example."

"He does seem to be working hard," Liz admitted.

"Good lad," said Roger, and leant towards her. "You tell him from us, now – if he'd like a bit of pocket money again, he could do weekends. Might do him good to have something other than school to think about. What do you think?"

"I think you're probably right," said Liz.

Marcus squeezed behind the bar with a tray of clean glasses. "We only want him back because we need a few new glasses – haven't broken enough recently! Joke! No, we've missed him, haven't we, Rog?"

Roger turned away. "As long as he hasn't forgotten how to pull a pint."

Liz went to clear some tables. She blew her nose and blinked hard. There are some more good ones, she thought.

The pub was becoming a hub of useful information.

"I won't have filthy gossip in my bar! Don't give a monkey's who's screwing who!" Roger would say to the regulars. "But if you want to pass a message on, we can usually put you in touch with someone useful – no use relying on the post any more."

He and Marcus had put up a notice board near the pub's entrance. For a while it had remained empty, but slowly messages began to appear. "Can anyone baby-sit Saturday night?" or "Lift to town needed, Thursday." Now and then there were letters; some in sharp new envelopes, and others grubby with travelling and handling, waiting for someone local to collect them or deliver them to a friend. "Bore da! Message for you down the Ferry," became a common greeting.

Liz always checked the noticeboard when she got to work, trying to keep it tidy and up to date. She threw away notes she knew had been dealt with, but letters hung about for longer.

One day she found she had missed a letter addressed to her. "Mrs. Elizabeth Patterson," it said, with her proper village address. She recognised the cramped hand, and tore the letter open. Yes, it was from Rodney. "… writing to inform you that, since your house is now apparently for sale, I have ceased my efforts to keep the front garden tidy. I've seen your husband and the boy, though we have not spoken. I must say that I thought some small remuneration would have been in order in view of my neighbourly help over the years, in these troubled times…"

Liz went into the bar and sat on a stool, still clutching the letter.

"Problem?" asked Roger.

"No!" Liz answered. "Well, yes – but I don't know what's happening – who's with him there."

Roger poured a large brandy and handed it to her. "Medicinal," he said.

Liz took a swig. She showed Roger the letter.

"Cheeky sod!" said Roger. "Is he making it up?"

"I don't know."

"Who, then?"

"Alfred?" said Liz. "Ben met them both in town – remember?"

"Not surprising the boy's looking down-in-the-mouth, then. Father's gone again and he's still worrying about that Alfred."

Marcus appeared with a plate of sandwiches. "Food," he announced. Roger went off to serve customers; Liz ate a sandwich and felt better.

"It's Alfred who's the real problem, isn't it?" said Marcus. "We can see you were okay without the husband…"

Liz was about to protest, but then had to agree – she was fine without Michael, and so were the children.

"Yes," she admitted. "But I'd like to know that Alfred is far away and won't come back. There's nothing I can do about that."

"Sounds to me as if it's confrontation time," he said.

"Well… I've talked to Michael already. And he ran away!" she said. "Why would he take Alfred, though?"

"Look, you need to know – and Ben needs to know

– that Alfred isn't a threat any more. Talk to your man and find out what he's playing at, and how that boy fits in – if he does."

"How do I to do that? I can't just phone any more. If I write I can't guarantee he'll actually get the letter, let alone read it."

"You'll have to go and see him, maybe" said Roger, stretching over to take empty plate and glasses.

"I can't!" Liz wailed. "How can I leave the children? I can't take them with me – they have to go to school. There's no transport!" She went quiet, seeing Roger and Marcus watching her.

"How did you get here?" Roger asked.

"By car," she said. "But there was petrol, then."

"And who has petrol now?" Roger asked.

"Well, Cyril, I suppose, but…"

"Black market," said Marcus.

Liz looked at him.

"No joke," said Marcus. "He gets petrol because he delivers food. He's not averse to selling a bit on the side."

Liz thought for a moment. "What about the children?"

"You're not going for months! I'm sure the estimable Mrs. Phillips could manage for a few days. The boy's nearly grown-up now, and young Kate's a sensible child."

Liz stopped. Kate was a sensible child. "Okay," she said in a small voice. "If I must…"

"You must," said Roger. "Now, go and make arrangements with Mrs. P. We'll sort the car out for you."

"Oh, but I must pay for that!" Liz said.

"Of course! We're not running a charity!" Roger growled.

"But you don't need to do it this very moment," Marcus said. "We can live on our fat for a few days. Joke!" he added, patting his belly.

When Ben and Kate asked her why she was going to London, she gave the obvious answers: sorting out finances and the house, generally tidying things up. She didn't mention Alfred.

"Alone?" asked Ben. "Are you sure that's safe?"

Liz realised he was thinking of his own dangerous journey. "I'll be in the car!" she reassured him. "I shan't be out in the open – don't worry!"

"Who will look after us?" asked Kate.

"Mrs. Phillip will come and stay and see you off to school. It won't be any different, really," said Liz. "She's a good cook," she added seeing Kate's face cloud.

"Okay," said Ben.

"Will you be long?" Kate asked.

"No," Liz answered. "I'm only going to help Daddy put everything in order. A couple of days at most."

"Are you going to bring him back?" Kate asked.

"He's not a sack of potatoes!" said Ben. "He'll come back when he can. He's very busy."

"I know," said Kate. "I'm going to start another story for Mrs. Phillips," and she went to find her exercise book.

"I just need to deal with a few things," Liz said,

seeing Ben looking at her.

"Okay," Ben answered. "But can't I come with you?"

"I'll be all right," Liz said. "You've got school."

"Yeah," said Ben. "But if Alfred's still around…"

"If," said Liz. "If…"

Next day, she said goodbye to a tearful Kate at the school gates.

"You are coming back, aren't you, Mummy? I mean, Ben's very cross sometimes…"

"Of course I am."

"But Daddy doesn't always come back, does he?"

"That's different!" Liz said. "Off you go. See you soon." She waved and blew kisses until Kate disappeared inside.

Back at the house she looked round for Ben, but he seemed to have gone already. She thanked Mrs. Phillips again. "I hope they won't be any trouble," she said.

"They usually save their worst behaviour for their parents, in my experience," said Mrs. Phillips. "They'll be fine!"

It was well after ten by the time Liz left. She'd packed an overnight bag, filled the tank and a can with contraband petrol to get her there and back, and put the goody bag the children had made for her on the passenger seat within reach – apples, biscuits, and two very thick cheese sandwiches.

"Because we didn't find much nice food on the way here," Kate explained.

"Neither did I," said Ben.

26

Liz drove through the village, ignoring the curious eyes following her progress, along the narrow tree-lined roads by the river, and onto the motorway. Lorries, vans and police cars sped past, but very few private cars.

When she felt hungry after a while, she turned off into a service station. Few cars again, and no other women in the cafeteria. She bought coffee, and returned to the car to eat one of her sandwiches.

She was getting really tired as she neared London, and put the radio on again. So far, there had been snippets from local stations, then, sentimental and supposedly uplifting music, and finally, real-life stories of how people were coping with their problems. Liz flicked it off crossly. She wanted to hear real facts – had the virus run its course? Were deaths really decreasing? Was Michael right in his blithe assertion that everything was getting back to normal? She wasn't sure what "normal" was, any more.

Central London, and it was beginning to get dark. She remembered when all the streets had blazed with light from shops, offices, and street lamps. But now all was gloom. The car's headlights showed boarded-up shop windows, locked metal grills, though there were still signs of break-ins – broken glass, and hoardings ripped away. Garish posters peeled from walls – "Save our medics!" they implored, or "Give us our lives back!" or, sadly, "Remember our Mum." Blocks of flats and office buildings, hastily evacuated in the hope of preventing the virus spreading, loomed blackly against the paler sky. Rubbish was piled up on street corners, black bags ripped open by scavenging foxes or feral pets, refuse strewn across pavement and road. Liz drove slowly – it was hard to see and the roads were full of potholes. An occasional figure scuttled along in the shadows. Now and then a near-empty bus rattled by, and she often had to pull over quickly to avoid an ambulance or police car that screeched dangerously near. Dust and old newspapers blew through the metal gates of underground stations. No one used the tube any more – it was too dangerous, crowding next to fellow travellers. Was this really what Michael had meant by "returning to normal"? Liz shivered. It had become a desolate place, this city. She was not happy to return.

Town softened into suburb. Still trees, branches stretching across the roads, and gardens, unkempt and wilding. Still no street lights. Many houses were boarded up and vandalised, gates broken, fences knocked down. Curtains muffled the windows, so no light – if there were any – could escape. Did people still live here? Or had they all run – like us, Liz thought – or died? She began to feel afraid. And still the ambulances and police cars shrieked past.

Then at last she was pulling up in front of the old house.

A For Sale board leaned sideways from the tall and straggly hedge. Dead rosebush sticks poked up through weeds and rubbish – old beer cans, plastic bottles, broken glass. A couple of windowpanes were cracked and bits of the stained glass in the front door were missing.

She sat in the car with the engine idling, summoning her courage for the next step. What if there'd been a burglary? Should she go straight in? Knock first? Maybe there was nobody there. Or she'd be ambushed as she got to the hall. Christ! Get out of the car! she told herself, turning off the ignition, and undoing her seatbelt. She brushed crumbs from her lap, reached for her bag and house keys and pushed open the gate, with its familiar clang. She banged loudly on the door and rang the bell. Silence. She tried again.

As she put her key in the lock, the hall light came on and the door was flung open.

Alfred.

"Still got your keys, then. What's all the racket for?" he said, as if she'd disturbed him at some urgent task. He was drunk.

"What the fuck are you doing here?" Liz said.

"Whoa!" he said. "Nice way to greet an old friend! How about, 'Alfred! How nice to see you! Shall we put the kettle on?'"

"Where's Michael?" she demanded. She marched past him. The place was filthy. The hall was strewn with bits of china and glass, ripped books, torn cushions, and empty wine bottles. A good portion of Michael's cellar, by the look of it.

"You did this?" Liz said.

Alfred looked down, as if he were ashamed for an instant. "Had a few mates over," he admitted. "You know…"

"No, I don't!" Liz yelled. "How did you get in?" She went into the sitting-room. Alfred followed. It was worse in there – curtains had been pulled down, the settee appeared to have been knifed, its stuffing poking out, and bottles from the drinks' cabinet lay on every surface, empty or oozing sticky dregs.

"Does Michael know? Where is he?" she asked.

Alfred turned away and started to pick up bottles. "He said I could stay here until I was fixed up," he said, with a touch of his old swagger. "Stay as long as I needed."

"I bet trashing the place wasn't part of the deal!"

"I was going to clear it up – I thought you were him, honest. I was just going to start." He brandished an empty gin bottle in her direction, and she jumped back. "Don't worry," he said. "I wouldn't hurt you – look, I'm tidying now."

He came nearer to her, and she could smell the alcohol on his breath.

"It's all right," he said. He reached out towards her with bottles in both hands.

Liz swung her bag at him and knocked the bottles away.

"There was some gin left in that one – we could have had a drink," he said, aggrieved.

"You must be mad!" As Liz leant forward to recover a bottle before it rolled under the settee, Alfred lunged. She felt her face scrape against the dust of the carpet and his knees on her back. She flailed about trying to turn round and beat him away. She was too breathless to scream. Who'd hear anyway?

"Won't hurt you," he said. "Don't want to hurt you."

Then suddenly Alfred was shouting "Get him off me!" He twisted and fell from her back as a furious figure yanked Alfred away. Liz rolled over and someone swung a bottle at Alfred's head. There was a clunk and Alfred slithered to the floor and lay still.

"How the hell did you get here?" Liz said, heaving herself upright.

"Just passing," said Ben. "Can't believe you didn't see me! I was in the boot up against the back seat. Just woke up," he added.

"Christ – what about Kate? Mrs Phillips? They'll be frantic!"

"No, no – I left them a note – put it on the kitchen table where they'd see it. Good thing I'm here, though?"

Liz hugged her son.

She knelt to check Alfred. "God. His head's bleeding – you hit him really hard!"

"I was trying to help you! But I can see his pulse,

look." Ben pointed at the small flutter under the pale skin.

"Thank god you were here – he's really strong. We ought to clean the wound, I suppose. Find a flannel or something, Ben. And some water."

Liz watched Alfred. In another time she'd have called the police, an ambulance. Now she could only wait. She didn't trust him even when he was unconscious. His breathing was regular; from time to time his eyelids flickered. "Alfred," she said. No response. She heard Ben banging about in the kitchen, then upstairs.

"Got a clean tea towel," he said as he came back. "Couldn't find any plasters; what about this pillow case?" He started to swab the wound on Alfred's forehead.

"I'll do that," said Liz

"I can do it," Ben said.

Alfred groaned and tried to sit up, waving off the cloth in Ben's hand. "Get him off me!"

"He's trying to help!" Liz said."

Alfred rolled over to sit up. "I wasn't going to hurt you. Well, I'm off then," he said, staggering to his feet. "Shan't stay where I'm not wanted."

"You can't go – you might be concussed," said Liz.

"Like you care!" Alfred lurched towards the sitting-room door, but collapsed onto the sofa.

"I don't," said Liz. "As soon as you can walk straight, you're out and that's that."

"What's going on here?" Michael strode into the room. "Some fool left the front door open."

"We came to see you, Dad," Ben said. "Alfred

attacked Mum, and I tried to stop him."

"He's wrecked the house, and drunk most of your wine, by the look of it – and he insists you asked him to stay."

"Well, I offered him a bed. I was going to put some work his way: the Department can always use people with a bit of spark."

"Who push people off cliffs?" said Ben. "Take hostages? Traffic humans?"

"What do you mean? The Welsh police let him go – no problem. He wasn't accused of anything."

"They don't have the time… or the people," Liz said.

"I am not part of your vendetta! I simply saw a young lad with a bit of spirit – gave him a bit of a hand."

"And this?" Liz waved a hand at the wreckage.

"I was going to clean it up, I told you," Alfred said.

"I'd have dealt with him," said Michael grimly.

Alfred raised his head and gazed at Michael. "You?" he jeered. "You can't even deal with your own family!"

Michael moved abruptly towards him.

"Leave him, Dad. He's only winding you up."

"Yeah," Alfred sneered. "That's what I'm good at – that's my trick. You needed a gofer," he said to Michael, " – and there I was! I got your family back and I looked after your boy before I even knew he was your boy – how clever was that? And where were you? Off up North. I thought I could do with a bit of that – extra rations, like – money, petrol –"

"For my family!" Michael said loudly.

"That'd be why you left them on their own in Wales!"

"I knew exactly where they were!"

"But we didn't know where you were," Liz couldn't help adding.

"See?" said Alfred. "You didn't give a toss about them, and there I was –"

"Cheeky little shit. I gave you – "

"A couple of dinners and a bed? So what!" He paused to tie the tea-towel round his head. "I'm going now. Had enough." He got up and turned to the door.

"You come back here! You're going nowhere until you've cleared up this mess!" Michael shouted.

"Leave him," said Ben again.

Michael leapt towards Alfred, who was stumbling into the hall and struggling with the latch. He jerked the front door wide open. A gust of air set the empty bottles rolling; a police siren screamed.

"That's going to be for you!" Michael said, grabbing at Alfred and missing. He lurched for Alfred again and shook him.

"You hurt my wife or my son again, and I'll…I'll…!"

"What? Those Cleaners know nothing about me," Alfred said. "Probably know more about you." He wrenched himself free as the sound of sirens got louder. He shouted over the noise. "Friends – just wanted to be friends!"

He staggered down the path and out of the gate.

27

From the doorstep, they watched Alfred weave his way into the road. Liz shouted in warning as a police car sped up the road, headlights blazing. Ben and Michael shouted above the siren, and Liz screamed – but Alfred lurched on. Brakes screeched. There was a stink of rubber, and a thud.

A bundle of shabby clothes flew up and flopped onto the ground. Bits of it protruded like sticks. A stream of blood spread across the road's surface.

Sudden quiet.

Then car doors opened and slammed. One of the Cleaners walked over to the family, as they stood framed in the light from the hall. Another Cleaner walked over to bang on Rodney's door, who popped out so quickly it was obvious he'd been watching.

"Very unfortunate," said one policeman. "Do you know him?"

"Nothing to do with me," Rodney said, coming to stand at his gate. "I only looked out to see if my neighbours were all right – I always try to keep and eye…"

"He was just leaving us when the accident occurred,"

said Michael, ignoring Rodney. "Friend of the family. I suppose you will deal with…?"

The Officer turned to the other policeman and shook his head. "No business of ours," he said. "We'll go back and report the incident, and the rest is up to you."

"But what about an ambulance?" Liz said. "Are you sure he's dead?"

"Oh, yes," said the officer. "He's dead all right."

"You can't leave a body in the middle of the road," said Rodney. "We can't have bodies left all over the place."

"Then I suggest you go back inside your own house and leave his friends to deal with it."

Rodney retreated. "I'll be watching," he called from the safety of his own doorstep.

"Interfering fool!" Michael muttered. He turned to the policemen. "So how do we… deal with the body? You aren't called Cleaners for nothing, surely? I can't believe such things don't fall into your remit…"

"Believe what you like," said the officer. "You deal with it. That's the way it is, now."

Michael protested "What are we supposed to do? Can't leave him there." He felt in his jacket to bring out a wallet thick with notes.

The Officer's face went red. "It's still illegal to bribe officers of the law."

"Just offering to pay for a job to be done, that's all," Michael bluffed. "What the hell are we supposed to do? It wasn't our fault!"

"Bury it," the officers said. They stepped carefully

round the body, returned to their car and drove away.

"Well!" said Michael. "God knows how people manage round here…"

"They're more helpful in Wales," said Liz. "So what next?"

"We need a piece of cloth," said Ben.

"Right. Michael, you go and find a sheet or a bedspread or something, and Ben and I will…"

"We'll manage," said Ben, patting his mother's arm.

Michael hesitated, then went back into the house.

"Are you all right with this, Ben?" Liz asked.

Ben nodded. "Done it before. How about you?"

"I'm okay," she said, and hand in hand, they crossed the road to where Alfred lay.

Ben remembered the feel of dead flesh, but Alfred's skin was till warm. Ben looked at his mother as they knelt to straighten out Alfred's broken body; they moved slowly and carefully, as if they were trying not to hurt him. Liz sniffed up tears and rubbed her wet face on her sleeve.

"He was so young," she said.

Michael came out with an old sheet, which he chucked over the body.

"Careful!" Liz cried.

"We need it under, not over," said Ben, taking up the sheet. "Then we lift him on to it."

"Done this before?" Michael scoffed.

Ben stopped, hands clenched on the sheet. "I thought Mum told you," Ben replied.

Michael shook his head. "I thought it was just a story…"

Ben and Liz stared at him.

"Come on, then – do you want me to pick him up?"

"No. Help me spread the sheet out," Ben said. "You take his ankles, and I'll take his shoulders…"

"Right." Michael's face was pale and sweaty.

"Now we wrap him up," said Ben, as soon as the body was centred on the sheet.

"I'll do it!" said Liz. She bent to fold the cloth round the body, tucking it in and under.

"You're not putting him to bed!" said Michael, maddened by her slowness.

"Oh, fuck off, Michael!" Liz said. "He needs some respect, even if…"

"I thought you both hated him."

"Doesn't matter," Ben interrupted. "He's dead. We're going to bury him. Mum, you go and open the back door, and Dad and I will carry him through to the garden."

Father and son carried Alfred's cocooned form towards the light from the front door. They edged the body through the hallway, kicking aside the mess of cushions and books and bottles, and into the darkness of the garden.

"Where?" Liz asked.

"Under the holly tree," Michael said. "It's darker there – less chance of anyone seeing us."

Ben didn't care who saw. "Find the spades, then," he told his father.

"How the hell should I know…?" his father began, but went to rummage in the shed. He returned with a fork, a large spade and a trowel. "I thought you could have a go with this," he said, turning to Liz, but she'd gone back inside.

The earth under the holly tree was heavy and thick with fallen leaves

Now the body was decently wrapped up, Ben forgot that it belonged to Alfred. He dug as he had dug at the Chocolate Farm, finding a rhythm, spade slicing into the earth, lifting and tipping the soil along the edge of the pit.

Michael was more haphazard. "Haven't done this for years," he said to Ben, pulling the fork out of the clay with effort, and breathing laboriously.

They worked for a long time in silence.

Eventually, Ben stopped. "Deep enough," he said.

"Thank god for that." Michael was panting. "Still, we made a good team, didn't we?"

"Not bad," Ben said.

"Have you finished?" came Liz's voice, quietly. "Only there's some food ready."

"Nearly," said Ben. He and his father picked up the body by shoulders and ankles, and placed it in the grave. They shovelled the earth back again, until Alfred was covered with dark, stony soil and dead leaves.

"Give us a hand, then," said Michael, and Liz crouched with the trowel, pushing the earth back into place.

They dropped their tools and looked down at the disturbed ground.

"Was he so bad?" Michael asked.

"Yes," said Ben. "You just never knew…"

"He was so young," said Liz again.

They went inside, and Michael jammed the broken back door shut.

"He's not going to get in, you know," said Liz, and Ben sniggered, and swayed on his feet.

"Food," said Liz, thrusting a tuna sandwich at him. "Are you sitting with us?" she asked Michael.

"Well, it is my house –"

"And mine, at the moment."

"Oh, for fuck's sake – can't you leave it alone for one moment? We'll sort it – that's what you came for, isn't it?"

Ben pushed his chair back, grabbed more sandwiches and some hard-boiled eggs, and went to eat in the sitting-room by himself. Then he realised he'd brought nothing to drink, so went back to the kitchen and ran the cold tap.

"Joining us after all?" Michael said, mocking.

"Leave him," said Liz. "It's not his fight."

"It's not anyone's fight," said Michael. "I only want things sorted properly, so we all know we're doing what's best for everyone."

"But we decided that in Wales!" said Liz.

"Let's see if he's changed his mind, now he's come back home, eh?"

Ben poured another glass of water and gulped it down. He sat back at the table, head in hands. He didn't want this conversation, now or any time. Why did they both have to be so dogmatic? He was quite happy to let things slither along as they always had, his father with one life, and they with theirs.

"Wales is home," he said, looking at both parents. "You know that, Mum. We had a helluva time getting there, and now it's home. We go to school. It's all sorted."

"A little Welsh comprehensive?" said Michael.

"The teachers are happy with Ben," said Liz.

"What the hell do they know! He needs a proper school…"

"It is a proper school!" said Ben. "So is Kate's. We're getting on all right, and we're okay there, actually…"

His father stood up abruptly, scraping his chair. He shrugged. "Well, you seem to have made up your minds! If that's how it is, then I'm off to bed. See you in the morning – I've got an early start."

"What exactly are you doing now?" Liz asked.

"Putting the finances to rights –"

"Ours?"

Michael sighed. "I don't think you've ever understood my job, have you?"

"Perhaps if you'd bothered to explain…"

Ben slid out of the kitchen and threw himself back on the sofa. He arranged some cushions round him to make a bed. He couldn't face his old bedroom.

The voices stopped.

He heard his mother clearing up in the kitchen, then her feet tiptoeing up the stairs, to Kate's room, he thought. Overhead he could hear his father moving about in the main bedroom.

So that was it, then.

And he slept.

28

He was woken by clattering in the kitchen.

"Come on," said his mother putting her head round the door. "Your Dad's been out to find some bread."

Ben stretched, and rolled off the sofa.

In the kitchen, his parents sat at either side of the table, spreading honey on their toast, and drinking milk-less instant coffee. Michael's briefcase was on the floor beside him.

"There's jam, too, if you don't mind scraping the mould off," said Michael.

They ate in silence for a while. Then Michael cleared his throat.

"You're not at a board meeting," said Liz. "Just tell him."

"I know already," said Ben, looking from one to the other.

His mother looked relieved; his father looked irritated.

"What do you know?" he asked.

"Oh, come on, Dad – I'm not stupid! You don't spend time with us – you and Mum don't talk… We've got different lives, now. Kate's used to you being away. So you're splitting up, right? It happens all the time."

"Not to us, it doesn't!" Michael protested. After a moment, he shrugged. Rising from the table he picked up his briefcase. He held his hand out to Ben, then, dropping the case, folded him into a clumsy hug. "I'll be in touch," he said. "You can come and visit here, when things are more normal – you might even learn to drive!"

Liz watched them both. "You'll be all right?" she said to Michael at last.

"Of course."

They moved together, and wrapped their arms round each other.

"Look after Kate," said Michael as he went towards the door.

"Of course," said Liz. "And Ben."

"He's too big to need looking after," said his father, aiming a mock punch at Ben's shoulder.

And he was gone.

Ben looked at his mother. She wasn't crying, in fact she looked calm, wiped clean.

"Shall we tidy up a bit?" he suggested.

"No!" said Liz firmly. "We'll leave that for your dad. We'll just do the kitchen, get our stuff together, then we're off – right?"

"I didn't bring anything," said Ben.

"Then you'll be really quick, won't you! Just give me a hand filling the car from the can in the back –"

"Did Cyril let you have all that?" asked Ben, amazed.

"With a bit of persuasion," said Liz. "And quite a lot of money!"

"I'll bet!" said Ben, and they laughed.

And in less than half an hour, they were on their way home. Home to Kate, and the house, and Wales.

Lightning Source UK Ltd.
Milton Keynes UK
UKHW022033051121
393447UK00010B/617